Note to Readers

While the Lankfords and Allertons are fictional families, John Hancock, General Lafayette, and other figures you will meet in this book were in Boston at the time of this story.

The Revolutionary War brought many changes to Boston. As James tells Paul, schools actually closed. Loyalist families left their homes and belongings in Boston to move first to New York City and later to Canada. And it took more than two years after the final battle before peace was officially declared.

While the Revolutionary War brought freedom to the United States, that freedom came at a high price to many families. That's one reason so many people fight to preserve our freedoms today.

☆ *The* ☆
AMERICAN
VICTORY

JoAnn A. Grote

BARBOUR
PUBLISHING, INC.
Uhrichsville, Ohio

For two special girls, my nieces,
Ashley and Alyssa Falvey

© MCMXCVII by JoAnn A. Grote.

ISBN 1-57748-159-3

Published by Barbour Publishing, Inc.
          P.O. Box 719
          Uhrichsville, Ohio 44683
          www.barbourbooks.com

 Member of the
Evangelical Christian
Publishers Association

Printed in the United States of America.

Cover illustration by Chris Cocozza
Inside illustrations by Adam Wallenta.

CHAPTER 1

A Welcome Surrender
Boston, Massachusetts—October 1781

Paul Lankford hurried to the door of his father's print shop. The fast clatter of wooden wheels and horses' hooves against cobblestones meant someone was quickly coming through the narrow Boston street. A handsome coach pulled by matched bay horses filled the street. Servants rode in front and behind, some black and some white. It had to be John Hancock's coach! What could he be doing in this quiet business street?

The coach stopped in front of the print shop. One of the servants opened the door, and John Hancock stepped out, adjusting his fancy long coat and ruffled shirt and sleeves.

Paul stared openmouthed as the great man came right to the print shop door, carrying a broadside in his hand. Mr. Hancock poked his head inside the shop, saw no adults inside, and turned back to Paul. "Is Mrs. Lankford about, lad?"

"N. . .no, sir. May I be of help?"

Mr. Hancock smiled that kind of smile adults give when they think a child is being silly. "I think I must speak to Mrs. Lankford. It's quite an urgent matter."

"I'm Paul Lankford, her son." Paul bowed slightly from the waist, more quickly than was proper. He'd been so surprised at Mr. Hancock's appearance that he'd forgotten to greet him like a gentleman! "I know I look young, sir, but I often help about the shop."

His cheeks grew hot as the great man looked him up and down. "I think I'd best wait for your mother."

"Joel!" Paul's call brought another boy to his side. Joel was six, two and one-half years younger than Paul. He had laughing brown eyes and black curly hair. They didn't look anything like brothers. Paul's hair was merely brown and straight.

"Run home and tell Mother Mr. Hancock wants to speak with her. Quick!"

Joel glanced at Mr. Hancock, then at his coach and servants, and raced up the street.

Wouldn't you know the most important man in Massachusetts would stop when Mother and her apprentice, James, were both out of the shop! But wait until Paul told his friends. Everyone in Boston knew who John Hancock was. Almost everyone in the world knew who he was, Paul guessed.

Paul watched as Mr. Hancock surveyed the print shop. One wall had yellowed broadsides and newspapers nailed upon it. BOSTON MASSACRE, BOSTON TEA PARTY, PORT BILL, SUFFOLK RESOLUTIONS: bold black letters at the top of old broadsides announced the stories that had led to the war the colonies were now fighting against the British.

The story of the war was on that wall as well. DECLARATION OF INDEPENDENCE read a paper that told of thirteen American colonies declaring themselves states, or countries, separate from Great Britain on July 4, 1776. John Hancock had signed that, Paul remembered, risking his life and his fortune by doing so.

Important battles headlined other papers: CONTINENTALS WIN BATTLE OF TRENTON read a paper from right after Christmas 1776; REDCOATS CAPTURE PHILADELPHIA said another from the spring of 1777.

Paul glanced about the office. It seemed dark and dreary with such a wealthy, important man in it, but it was the same as always. It smelled of ink and leather and paper. One wall held all the letters, called type, used to print the newspaper. Each letter had its own wooden box. There was a separate box for capital letters and another for small letters. Shelves held supplies and paper. The wooden printing press filled most of the room.

Mr. Hancock pulled a gold watch from his pocket. "Do you think your mother will be long? I have an appointment to keep."

"It will take her a few minutes, sir. She's at home."

"Perhaps I can leave this with you. Write down what I tell you, so you can be sure to tell her correctly." He hesitated. "Do you know how to write?"

"Yes, sir." Paul pulled the cork from a stoneware ink jar and stuck a quill into the black ink.

"I received this only an hour ago. We'll need broadsides made up to spread the news."

"Yes, sir."

Mr. Hancock handed him the paper. Paul glanced at the bold black letters at the top. "Sir, this says Cornwallis has surrendered to General Washington!"

"So it does, lad." Mr. Hancock beamed.

"Does this mean the war is over?"

"Almost, almost. Now don't forget to tell Mrs. Lankford that I need these broadsides first thing in the morning. If she can't print the order in time, you must get a message to my aide, and we'll find another printer."

"We can do it, sir."

"If you do, I may have another printing job for you soon. I'm planning a dinner and ball to celebrate the surrender and a fireworks display on the common near my home. I'll need a broadside for the public invitation."

Paul barely noticed the famous man leave. He scanned the paper quickly, his heart leaping at the report of General Cornwallis and seven thousand men surrendering to General George Washington. Paul's father was fighting with Washington's army. Had he seen the surrender?

It was already late in the day. Mother and James would be hard pressed to get all the broadsides printed by morning. Paul decided to start setting up the press.

He grabbed the iron composing stick. Taking the letters he needed from their boxes one by one, he put them in order on the stick, with a blank metal piece between each word. He remembered to put the letters on backward, so they would be in the right order when they were printed. He bit his bottom lip as he worked, concentrating hard. The composing stick held a number of lines of type. It was almost full when his mother entered the shop. Joel followed right behind.

Eliza Lankford held four-year-old Rachel's hand and propped three-year-old David on one hip. Wisps of hair had escaped from her large mobcap-style bonnet and played about her face. Excited eyes glanced about the room, then dimmed before looking at Paul. "Did I miss Mr. Hancock?" She was panting, like she'd run all the way.

Paul nodded.

"We could have used that order. Did he say what he wanted?"

Paul grinned and nodded at the paper lying beside him where he could see it while composing. "He wants the broadsides of this first thing tomorrow morning."

"Tomorrow morning!" she wailed. "We'll never make it."

She set David down and picked up the paper. "Paul, Cornwallis surrendered!" She threw her arms about his neck.

His composing stick tilted. "Careful!"

"You've already started composing the broadside. What would I ever do without you? Now, where did that James get off to?"

"You sent him for more paper, remember?"

"Oh, that's right. I'm just so excited about this order, and the surrender!"

"Maybe you should do the composing, Mother," Paul suggested as he finished the first composing stick. "You're quicker at it than I am. I'll cut the paper."

He didn't usually like working in the print shop. He'd rather be at his Uncle Ethan's shipyard. But he'd been helping at the shop ever since he could remember. He'd had to help, with his father off fighting the war and his mother running the shop with only the apprentice, James, to help.

Even though he'd rather be by the harbor in the open air with the bustle of the wharves about, Paul was proud of what he could do in the print shop. He could read better than any of the boys in his class at school, even most of the older boys. He could write better, too. His mother had taught him from the Bible and the newspapers.

There was a tug at his leather apron. "Davey hungry."

His mother spun around, the half-filled composing stick in one arm. "I forgot about dinner. I was only starting it when Joel came with the message that Mr. Hancock was awaiting me. Joel, you run home and bring back that fresh loaf of bread. Bring some apples, too. That should get us through the evening."

Another tug at Paul's apron. "Davey's hungry."

Paul bit back an impatient answer. "Joel will be back with your dinner soon. Why don't you and Rachel practice your horn-books while you wait?"

Davey sat down hard on the hearth with a sigh. A second later he jumped up, craned his neck to see the back of his breeches, and brushed at his bottom with the palm of one chubby hand.

Paul grinned. Davey was wearing his first pair of breeches. Until he stopped wearing diapers, he'd worn a dresslike frock, like all little boys. He was very proud of those breeches!

"Rachel, get the hornbooks down, won't you?" Paul asked, since Davey had already forgotten about them.

The wooden, paddle-shaped hornbooks hung by leather ties beside the fireplace. Rachel reached for them, her black curls so like Joel's tumbling down her back.

"Don't sit too close to the fire," he warned her and Davey.

"It's too dark to read the hornbooks if we don't," Rachel protested.

It was almost candlelighting time, Paul realized with surprise. It wasn't quite dark outside yet, but it was that in-between time when it seems light outdoors but dark inside. He'd been so excited with Mr. Hancock's order that he hadn't even noticed it growing darker.

He set aside the paper, lit a candlewick at the fireplace, and used it to light other candles about the room. Rachel and Davey's voices formed a singsong background to his work as they repeated the alphabet.

A tin ship chandelier hung from the ceiling near the press. His mother liked it because the candlelight reflected off the tin and made more light than a candle in a normal candleholder. The rope that held it in place was wrapped around a piece of metal attached to the wall. Paul unwound it and lowered the chandelier until he could easily light its candles. Then he pulled on the rope until it hung high above them again.

James returned as Paul was fastening the rope. He carried a load of paper. Paul helped him unload the rest of the paper from the wooden wheelbarrow outside the front door, explaining about Mr. Hancock's broadside while they worked.

James was a pleasant, blond, sixteen-year-old young man with arms muscular from years of working the press. He started right in helping without a word of complaint, just like always. While Paul continued cutting paper, James took a yoke and wooden buckets and went to the nearby city pump for the water they would need.

Minutes later Joel came back with the round of bread and a small basket full of apples. He tore chunks of bread off and gave pieces to Davey and Rachel. Paul, James, and Mother said they would eat later. They were too busy to eat.

Mother finally laid the last line of type for the paper in the press's wooden case. Paul leaned against the press and watched as she made sure the lines were straight and the margins even.

"That's it. We're ready to run the proof."

James was busy dampening paper for the print job.

Paul took two wool and leather balls by their wooden handles and inked them well. Holding one in each hand, he beat the balls against the letters to spread ink over the type.

When the letters were all inked, James laid a damp sheet of paper on the press stone. Then he grabbed the wooden handle that was attached to the press at shoulder height and pulled it as hard and quickly as he could, twice. His hard pulls rolled the paper under the screw that pressed the letters against it to make the newspaper.

Paul read the printed page aloud slowly. His mother followed along on the paper Mr. Hancock had given them. Whenever they found a mistake, they changed the type to make it right. When they were done, Mother laughed and pointed at the hearth. "Look!"

Rachel and Davey were curled up asleep, as cozy as two cats, in front of the hearth.

"I'd best get a blanket for them from home. James and Paul, start printing the broadsides while I'm gone."

By the time she was back, damp, freshly printed papers hung from racks near the ceiling to dry. The room smelled of wood smoke from the fireplace and wet paper and ink from the broadsides.

A few minutes later the door opened again. Uncle Ethan, with his round face and shaggy gray eyebrows, entered with his eleven-year-old daughter, Maggie. Candlelight danced off her blond curls and excited green eyes.

"You'll never guess what's happened!" Maggie said in her usual exuberant manner.

Ethan smiled and shook his head. "Once we'd heard, Maggie

wouldn't rest until we told you."

"Cornwallis has surrendered at Yorktown!" Maggie burst out. Paul and James laughed.

"We know!" Paul held up a freshly printed broadside.

Maggie's excitement died when she read the bold black letters at the top. "I thought we had news for you for a change. You always know everything that happens before the rest of Boston."

Paul had never thought of it that way before. To him, printing news was just his family's work, work he didn't like.

Maggie grabbed his arm. "Isn't it wonderful? I always knew we'd win the war! Aren't you proud of your father? He's fought since the first battle at Lexington, six and one-half years ago. Not many men can say that, even the most red-hot patriots."

"Of course I'm proud of him."

Paul was proud of his father. Still, he sometimes wished for a father like Maggie's instead. Uncle Ethan owned Foy Shipping Company. He hadn't fought in the war, but he'd given a ship to the Continentals to use for a warship and given money to help Congress pay the war debts. Uncle Ethan didn't go off for years to fight and leave his wife and oldest son to run the business and raise the rest of the children, either.

"Now that the war's over, your father will be coming home. Aren't you excited?" Maggie's question interrupted Paul's thoughts.

"Your father may not get home right away," Uncle Ethan said before Paul could answer. "Congress may not let the army go home until a treaty is signed."

Paul scowled up at him. "What is a treaty?"

"That's the agreement between the leaders of the countries that the fighting is over."

"I thought that's what the surrender was."

"The surrender was agreed to between some of the armies' leaders. Even though they agreed and Cornwallis's men are now prisoners, until the peace treaty is signed, the British still control Charleston, South Carolina, and Savannah in Georgia, as well as New York. They may decide to continue fighting."

"Do you think they will?" Mother asked.

"No," Uncle Ethan replied. "I don't believe they could win a war against us without Cornwallis's army."

Maggie crossed her arms and gave a sharp nod of satisfaction that set her curls bouncing. "Of course they couldn't. The Yankees are the best army in the world."

Uncle Ethan grinned. "I'm not sure about that, but God has been with us, helping us in this war. He gave us a great military leader in George Washington."

"How long before the treaty is signed?" Paul asked.

"It could take months. Our Congress will send representatives to talk with representatives from England, France, Spain, and Holland—all the countries that fought in this war—and they will decide what the treaty will say."

After Uncle Ethan and Maggie left, Mother, Paul, and James went back to work on the broadsides. Joel even helped by hanging up the paper to dry when it came off the press.

But Paul's excitement about the surrender had worn off. All night while he inked letters and placed damp papers on the press stone, he thought about his father coming back from the war. He wasn't sure he wanted his father home to stay. He'd only seen him a few times in the last six and one-half years. Whenever his reenlistment was up, Father would come home for a few days or weeks and then go back to the army.

Guilt flooded Paul. He should be excited his father might be coming home. He should be glad his father hadn't been killed or wounded in the war, or taken prisoner like Maggie's brother Charles had been for a short while. Besides, wouldn't it be nice to have his father running the business? Then his mother wouldn't need his help here or with his brothers and Rachel as much. He could spend more time at Uncle Ethan's shipyard.

It was almost two in the morning before the last broadside came off the press. Pride filled Paul's chest. Mr. Hancock would have his broadsides in the morning as Paul had promised.

James carried Davey home, and Mother carried Rachel. Joel and Paul stumbled along beside each other, each carrying a tin-and-glass lantern to light their way through the dark, crooked streets.

All the way home Paul remembered that Uncle Ethan had said it could be months before his father came home. Months. He shouldn't be glad about that, but he was.

A week later, Paul was helping James print the broadsides announcing Mr. Hancock's fireworks celebrating the surrender. Davey, Rachel, and Joel played underfoot as usual, while Mother went to the market.

Half a dozen old men with nothing better to do stood beside the fireplace arguing about the new Congress. They often met at the print shop because it was here they would hear the latest news.

The arguing among the men today was nothing compared to when Paul's father came home between enlistments. Then the shop was always filled with people arguing politics. His father was always in the middle of them, with his laughing brown eyes and convincing voice. That is, for the few days he was home before he went back to the war.

Paul didn't pay much attention to the arguing men. He and James were too busy working. He still hoped they might get done early enough for him to run over to the shipyard. He never could understand why his father chose to be a printer when a man could do something as exciting as build ships.

His father didn't actually run the newspaper, Paul thought, hanging up a sheet of paper to dry, then turning to ink the letters again. Sure his father sent back letters from the war to Paul's mother to print in the newspaper, but his work was being a soldier, not a printer.

Joel, Davey, and Rachel were playing drummer boys. They marched circles around the press, singing "Yankee Doodle" at the top of their lungs. Davey sang "Yankee Doodoo." Paul had made drums for them by stretching scraps of sailcloth over hollow pieces of wood he'd found at Uncle Ethan's shipyard.

Paul didn't even look up when the door opened again, the brass bells above it ringing to announce a visitor.

The room went still except for the sound of Paul pounding the ink-soaked leather and wool balls against the metal letters. He looked up to see who had entered to cause the sudden quiet. The balls fell from his hands. He stared at the tall man standing in the doorway in the rumpled Continental officer's blue uniform.

His father was home.

CHAPTER 2
Father's News

The men burst into shouts of welcome and hurried across the room to welcome Will Lankford back to Boston. A returned soldier from Washington's army! Had he been at Yorktown? Had he seen Cornwallis's army surrender?

Joel, Davey, and Rachel stopped beside the fireplace and watched, curious.

Paul's stomach churned and he felt his face grow hot. He hadn't expected his father home so soon. He picked up the balls and went back to inking the letters.

The bells rang again, and Paul's mother entered. She stood in the doorway, staring at Father. Paul looked around. Was he the only one who noticed her? The men still surrounded Father.

Paul crossed the room, ducked beneath one of the old men's elbows, and yanked on his father's sleeve. "Mother's here."

"Eliza!" Father called over the men's heads.

The men filed out, assuring their friend that they'd be back in the morning.

Father held out his hands. "Eliza." She hurried to him. "It's so good to see you again."

"You're home." Her eyes shone, and she smiled up at him.

He held his arms wide and grinned at Paul. "Isn't anyone going to welcome their father home?"

Paul set the balls down on the press, wiped his hands on his ink-stained leather apron, and crossed the room slowly. His chest hurt a bit as he held out his hand. "Welcome home, Father."

Father laughed and shook his hand. "Looks like you're turning into quite the printer, son." He looked over Paul's head. Joel, David, and Rachel were standing in front of the fireplace, staring wide-eyed at their father. "Won't you come say hello?"

They just huddled closer together.

Paul knew how they felt. They didn't want to be friendly to this man they barely knew. Still, he was their father and they owed him respect. He took Rachel and David's hands. "Come say hello to Father."

Instead of walking with him, they each tried to clutch one of his legs. Paul looked at his father. "I guess they're afraid."

Father walked across the room and knelt in front of them. "I'm your papa. You don't need to be afraid of me." He held out his arms to Rachel. She scooted behind Paul.

"Don't rush them, Will," Mother said. "They need some time to get used to you again. It's been almost a year. Rachel was only three when you were home last time and Davey only two."

Father stood up, shaking his head. "How you've all grown!"

Paul hated when adults said that. It was as if they expected children to stay short forever.

His father dug in the pack he'd had on his back when he arrived. A moment later he pulled out a wooden fife. He placed it to his lips and played a couple bars of "Yankee Doodle." Then he held it out toward the children.

"Look what I've brought you. One of my friends carved it while we sat around the campfire. There's only one, so you'll have to share."

While Paul watched jealously, Joel stepped forward just far enough to grab the flutelike instrument. He stepped back quickly.

Joel tried to play it. All that came out was a windy sound.

Father laughed. "Keep practicing. You'll get the hang of it."

"We didn't expect you back so soon," Mother said, her eyes shining and her cheeks pink with joy. "We thought the army wouldn't be allowed to go home until the peace treaty was signed."

"The war men have to stay until then," Father said.

Paul knew the war men were the troops who had agreed to be soldiers until the end of the war like his uncle Stephen, who worked as a doctor among the troops and was then planning on attending the new medical school at Harvard University. He always thought of his father as a war man, even though he only enlisted for a year or so at a time.

"My last enlistment term was over the end of October," Father continued. "With Yorktown and Cornwallis's surrender behind us, I decided to come home and see my family for a couple weeks. It looks like peace is here, but until the treaty is signed, there could be more fighting. It's no time for a soldier to quit. I've been in the Continental army from the beginning, and I plan to be in it at the end."

Paul saw the disappointment on his mother's face. He knew she'd hoped Father was home for good this time.

Anger flashed through him. He went back to work to hide his feelings. He smashed the balls against the letters as hard as he could. It made him feel better to hit something. It made a little of the anger go away.

Why couldn't his father stay home? Paul and his mother always had to run the shop and take care of his brothers and sister. Wasn't that his father's job? There were lots of soldiers. Paul and his brothers and sister had only one father.

He wished he dared tell his father what he thought, but boys didn't speak to their fathers or any other adults that way. Even if they barely knew their fathers. Even if their fathers were one hundred percent wrong.

Father grinned at Mother. "How do you think the *Boston Observer's* readers would like an eyewitness report of Cornwallis's surrender?"

She tucked a hand under his arm and smiled up at him. "They'd love it, I'm sure."

"They certainly would, Mr. Lankford." James stepped up eagerly.

"James!" Will shook James's hand vigorously. "Good to see you're still with us. Eliza says you'll be a fine printer one day."

"Thank you, sir."

James's father had been killed in the war. Was he thinking that his own father wouldn't be coming home from the war? The thought made Paul ashamed of the harsh feelings he had toward his own father, but it didn't make them go away.

"There's nothing the readers like more than a report from a soldier that's been at a battle or soldier's camp," James said.

"They flock here when news gets around that Mrs. Lankford's received a letter from you."

Father pulled folded, wrinkled sheets of paper from his worn blue-and-red uniform pocket. "No letter this time. Just what I wrote down about what I heard and saw at the surrender." He handed it to James. "Think you'll be done with Hancock's broadsides in time for us to print this tonight?"

"Yes, sir!"

Father removed his officer's jacket and pulled a leather apron from a wooden peg on the wall. Then he grabbed a composing stick and began arranging letters.

James, Paul, and Mother went back to work on the handbills.

Every once in a while, Joel managed a squeak or two on the fife that was almost musical. Paul noticed the drums he'd made had been set aside. Rachel and Davey were fascinated with the fife. Joel let them try playing, but they were worse at it than he was.

The bells over the door rang again. "Welcome home, William!" A moment later Father and Paul Revere were pumping each other's hands and pounding each other on the back, grins filling their faces. Even though Mr. Revere was at least fifteen years older than Father, they'd always been good friends. Mr. Revere even had a son, Joshua, who was only about a year younger than Paul. Sometimes the two boys would float wooden boats together on the town's ponds.

"Good to see you, Paul," Father said. "Or perhaps I should say, Lieutenant Colonel Revere. Are you still in charge of the fort at Castle Island in Boston Harbor and the American soldiers there?"

"Until the peace treaty is signed," the large, ruddy-faced man replied. "And you, friend. Were you at Yorktown? Did you see the surrender?"

Father leaned back against the wooden letter boxes with his arms folded across his chest and told them all what it had been like when the famous British general, Lord Cornwallis, had surrendered over seven thousand British and German troops to General Washington.

"It's only thanks to the Lord's help Cornwallis and his troops didn't get away," Father stated. "They were camped in Yorktown on a peninsula surrounded on three sides by water. Our friends, the French, were in the harbor, so the British couldn't leave by sea. Washington and the Continentals were guarding the only way to leave by land.

"Cornwallis and his men tried to escape during the night. It was a calm, pleasant evening, and he began sending his troops across the river. Some had already landed when suddenly a violent storm started. The wind and rain were so bad that most of the boats filled with British troops were driven down the river and couldn't land at all. The next day Cornwallis's men finally made it back to York, but didn't make their escape."

"The sudden storm is another in a long line of wonders the Lord has sent to help the Americans during this war," Paul Revere said.

Father and Mother nodded.

What wonders were they talking about? Paul hoped he would remember to ask them one day. He knew better than to interrupt adults when they were visiting.

Father continued his story. "The next day, General Washington sent terms for surrender to Cornwallis by two of his aides. Cornwallis agreed."

"A glorious day for us, but a bitter one for Britain," Mr. Revere said, shaking his head.

"About noon on October 19, we lined up along the road to

receive the British troops, the Americans on one side and the French on the other. General Washington on his horse sat at the head of the line. Many of the Continentals didn't have uniforms, and many were dressed in nothing but rags, but every American had a smile on his face! The line went on for over a mile.

"It was almost two o'clock before the redcoats came out. Lord Cornwallis had ordered every man to have a new uniform. But the bright red coats and white breeches and vests didn't put any smiles on their faces as they marched down that long line between the American and French troops. They walked slowly, their muskets against their shoulders, their drummer boys beating a British march. The Germans joined them, of course."

Paul remembered the British had hired German soldiers to fight alongside them. The Germans were tough soldiers.

"Is it true Cornwallis never showed up?" Mr. Revere asked.

Father nodded. "It's true. He sent General O'Hara instead. General O'Hara walked with his horse at the head of the redcoats. When he reached General Washington, he mounted his horse, took off his hat, and apologized to Washington, saying Cornwallis was too ill to come.

"In the traditional sign of surrender, General O'Hara then tried to present his sword to the French commander. Evidently it was too much for the British to think they had to surrender to Americans, people they used to rule. The French commander refused the sword, and General O'Hara then offered it to General Washington.

"Since General O'Hara was only a substitute for Cornwallis, Washington wouldn't accept his sword. Instead Washington pointed to our General Lincoln. If you'll remember, General Lincoln had to surrender his sword to General O'Hara last year when the British conquered Charleston, South Carolina."

"What happened next?" Mother asked.

"The redcoats were directed to a large field at the end of the line. As they reached the field, the British platoon officers ordered their men to ground arms, and the soldiers left their muskets. The Continentals played 'Yankee Doodle.' The redcoats played the song, 'The World Turned Upside Down.'"

The British must think the world had been turned upside down, Paul thought while the room filled with laughter. After all, the British were considered the most powerful army and navy in the world, and they'd had to surrender to the Americans, who had very little army training, poor weapons, and no navy at all when the war began. The British must feel like the tough-talking school bully Andrew would feel if he lost to a skinny little kid in a fight.

Later, when Mr. Revere had left, James and Paul cleared the press of the handbill type. Then Father set up the type for the newspaper.

Paul reached for his leather and wool inking balls, but Father grabbed them first. Paul stepped back out of his father's way. Father hadn't even seemed to notice him!

Father inked the letters and jerked the wooden handle twice to print the proof. He was reading the damp printed sheet when Maggie ran in, her blond curls flying from beneath the large white bonnet edged with lace and tied by a ribbon beneath her chin. In her hand was an envelope.

"We've had a letter from Uncle Cuyler." She stopped abruptly and stared at Father. "Uncle Will, you're home!" She flew across the ink-stained wooden floor and threw her arms about his waist.

Father laughed and hugged her back. "Thank you for the nice welcome, Maggie. My, but you're growing into a pretty young thing."

Paul's chest ached as he watched them. Maggie was gladder

than he had been to see his own father.

"Oh!" Maggie's cheeks turned pink. "I forgot!" She spread her skirt and curtsied.

"Did you say you have a letter from Uncle Cuyler, Maggie?" Mother asked.

"Yes. Here it is."

Mother held out her hand for the letter, but Maggie didn't notice. She handed the letter to Father.

Father must not have seen Mother's hand, either, Paul thought. He was taking the letter out of the envelope that had Uncle Cuyler's familiar scrawl on the front.

Uncle Cuyler was Uncle Ethan and Grandmother Lankford's brother. He sent his letters to Uncle Ethan, knowing that Uncle Ethan would share his letters with the rest of the family. Paul's mother usually read the letters out loud to the rest of the family. Did she mind that Father was reading the letter instead?

Uncle Cuyler and his family were Loyalists. They'd lived in Boston until 1776. That year General Washington had forced the redcoats to leave Boston. The Loyalists, who were on the side of the British in the war, left with the redcoats. Now Uncle Cuyler's family lived in New York, along with thousands of other Loyalists. Many of the Loyalists had joined the British army and fought against the American Continentals, but Uncle Cuyler was a doctor and didn't like to fight.

Even though Cornwallis had surrendered in Virginia, the redcoats under General Howe were still in charge of the city of New York, Paul remembered. That's why so many Loyalists lived there. It was safe there for the Loyalists with the British troops.

Father didn't read Uncle Cuyler's letter aloud like Mother always had. Instead he just told them bits of what Uncle Cuyler had said.

Father looked up from the letter. "Uncle Cuyler says he and New York have heard of Cornwallis's surrender. I bet the general in charge of the redcoats in New York didn't like that bit of news!"

"What else does he say?" Mother asked.

Paul noticed his father still didn't hand her the letter to read. Instead he folded it and handed it back to Maggie.

"He says if the surrender truly means peace, he's glad for those of the family who are Patriots, like us. He asked about me, too, and said he hoped I was still well and would be joining you soon." Father grinned.

"Is that all?" Paul asked.

Maggie said, "Uncle Cuyler doesn't know what will happen to his family if General Howe and the redcoats leave New York. He doesn't know where the Loyalists can go to be safe." She laughed. "Maybe the Continentals will make the Loyalists prisoners of war, like they did Cornwallis's army."

Paul knew Maggie was a strong Patriot. He was, too. His mother and Uncle Ethan talked about Uncle Cuyler and his family a lot. Paul didn't remember them. He hadn't been quite three when they'd left Boston.

Still, he didn't like to think of anyone having no place to go where they could feel safe. Besides, Uncle Cuyler was Uncle Ethan's brother. What if it were his own brother, Davey, who didn't have a safe place to live?

"They'd like us to pray for them and the other Loyalists," Father said.

Paul decided he'd pray. Would God answer?

CHAPTER 3
The Decision

Paul walked happily beside Uncle Ethan through the bustle and noise of the shipyard. He didn't even mind the chill December wind that stung his cheeks and pulled at his hat.

A French man-of-war rose high above them. Thirty large timbers supported the boat, holding it upright in the yard. The workers had taken it out of the harbor to ready it for more ocean travel.

Paul dropped his head back and looked up as far as he could. He counted the wooden shutters on the lower decks. He knew that behind each shutter was a cannon. "It has sixty-four cannons."

"Yes, it's a large warship. Do you remember what I told you a shipwright must consider when building a man-of-war that's different from a merchant ship?"

"It must be built for speed, and its lowest cannons must ride four to five feet above the water."

"Very good!"

All of Rochambeau's four thousand men and his ships were in Boston. They'd arrived the first week of December and would be leaving before the end of the month. French flags atop the warships and transports brightened the harbor.

The ships were here to be repaired and graved before going back to France or on to the West Indies, where France was fighting another war. Refitting the ships was keeping Uncle Ethan's shipyard busy.

The air was filled with the strong smell of brown stuff, but Paul was used to it. Brown stuff was made of pitch, tar, and brimstone. Workers were busy all along the ship, spreading the brown stuff on the hull that would ride beneath the water. Paul knew that the brown stuff was needed to keep the wood from rotting. Above that, right below the part of the ship that rode above the water, they were spreading tallow and lime.

"Is this one of General Rochambeau's ships?"

"Yes."

"Then it was at Yorktown. It was with the French navy that kept Cornwallis from escaping by sea." Paul's heart beat a little faster. "I wish General Rochambeau had come to Boston with his men. It would have been fun to see such a famous general."

"General Lafayette is in town. Perhaps you'll see him."

Paul nodded. "But he doesn't command ships like General Rochambeau. Lafayette only commands army men on land."

"It's too bad you feel that way." Uncle Ethan caught his hands behind his back and pretended to be very interested in watching one of his men spreading brown stuff. "We're having Lafayette to dinner in a few days. We're inviting your father and mother, since your father was a Continental officer. I thought you might like to come over with them before the dinner begins and meet Lafayette. But if you'd rather not. . ."

Paul's heart thumped hard against his chest. "Of course I want to meet Lafayette! I only said. . .I mean. . ."

Ethan laughed and clapped Paul on the back. "I know what you meant."

"Do you think Father and Mother will let me come? I always have to watch my brothers and Rachel when they go anywhere."

They must let me go, they must! Paul thought.

"I'll talk with Will. I'm sure we can arrange something so you can get away for a short while."

"Thank you!" It didn't seem enough to just say thank you. Imagine meeting General Lafayette! Everyone knew he was General Washington's favorite officer. People said Washington loved him as a son.

"It was Lafayette who went to France and convinced the king to send Rochambeau and his fleet to help America, wasn't it? Cornwallis wouldn't have had to surrender if it weren't for Lafayette!"

"That's true," Uncle Ethan agreed.

What would Paul's friends think when they found out he'd met Lafayette?

"This is quite a ship, isn't it?" Uncle Ethan's question brought Paul's attention back to the shipyard.

"Do you think it's been in battle?" Paul asked. "Do you think it's fired those cannons at other ships? Do you think it's been fired upon by other ships?"

Uncle Ethan studied the ship, then nodded. "It's not a new ship." He pointed at the top deck, where lighter wood filled a section of rail, and at another area of lighter wood on a lower deck. "You can see where it's been repaired. Likely an enemy's cannon balls landed there. What kind of wood is best to protect a man-of-war against cannon balls?"

"Oak," Paul answered promptly.

"Correct again!"

They stepped around a large barrel of brown stuff. The smell almost made Paul's eyes water. But he liked the smells of the shipyard: the timber, the saltwater, and even the brown stuff.

He loved the excitement of seeing new ships being built, old ships being mended, or the bottoms of ships being graved. He loved the sounds of pounding and sawing and men yelling at each other while they hauled timbers or pulled a ship into stocks.

"This is my favorite place in the whole world," Paul said.

Uncle Ethan grinned down at him. "Mine, too." He was a large man with a round face and eyes that seemed to see everything that was going on around him. Paul knew his white wig that curled above the ears and tied into a club in back hid an almost bald head.

To the men who worked in the shipyard and to the men who governed Boston, Uncle Ethan was an important businessman. Paul thought he seemed more like a friendly grandfather.

"I wish I could stay and work with you all day instead of going to school," Paul said.

"You can't build ships without understanding the way God

made things work in the world. People who design ships, or buildings, or bridges aren't adding two plus two every day, but they are working with the laws of mathematics. Those are some of the laws God created to make the world work."

Paul had never before thought of school helping him make his dream of designing and building ships come true.

"Are you enjoying having your father home for a bit?" Uncle Ethan asked.

"Yes, sir." Paul didn't look at his great-uncle. Instead he studied the ship even harder. He didn't want Uncle Ethan to see that he wasn't really enjoying having his father back.

"What have you been doing together?"

Paul shrugged, his shoulders lifting his worn brown wool coat. "Not much."

"Have you talked about what each of you has been doing while he was gone?"

Paul kicked at a broken seashell. "Usually he talks about convincing Congress to pay the soldiers and what the new government should be like. I don't care much about that stuff, but I try to be polite and listen."

Uncle Ethan patted his shoulder. "That's good."

Paul's father had taken him along on some visits to friends in the evenings after school. Paul was glad his father wanted him around, but he was bored by the adults' talk. The only thing his father ever asked Paul was "How was school today?" or "What did you learn in school today?"

Paul didn't even talk to his father about his dream of building ships. He didn't think his father would understand. Besides, his father would just be leaving to go back to the army soon. Paul was sure that if he and his father became better friends it would only hurt more when his father left again.

Paul and Uncle Ethan walked around the ship's wide stern, being careful to avoid puddles of brown stuff that might stick to their shoes.

"We must urge our men in Congress to raise money to pay our soldiers."

Paul jerked his head around at the sound of his father's voice. Sure enough, there stood his father in the middle of a dozen ship carpenters. Some leaned on tools while they listened. Some sat on logs.

"The troops have faithfully fought for our freedoms." Father pounded a fist into the palm of his other hand. "It's only fair Congress pay them as soon as possible. They have families to care for, just like us."

A ship's carpenter stepped forward. Large arms bulged beneath his coat. "What good would it do our soldiers for Congress to be payin' them? The money Congress prints isn't worth anything!"

The men in the group nodded and murmured agreement.

"Then Congress needs to raise money with taxes."

Another man stood up. "Congress doesn't have the right to tax anyone."

He was right. The Congress had passed the Articles of Confederation earlier that year. The Articles were a list of things all the new states had agreed to. It said that Congress could make peace, declare war, make treaties, and print money. It couldn't keep states from printing money, it couldn't regulate trade, and most important, it couldn't tax people.

Father spoke louder than the muttering crowd. "Then it's up to you and me to convince the man representing Massachusetts in the Congress that we need an amendment. The states haven't the money to pay the soldiers or to pay our other war debts."

"Taxes are one of the reasons we fought this war!" yelled one of the carpenters. "We don't want taxes!"

"We fought because taxes were being levied on us by people we didn't choose to represent us," Father reminded him. "Now we choose our representatives. It's only fair we pay our part of the war bills."

"We have our own bills to pay," said a man leaning on his axe.

Father spoke very quietly. The men stopped muttering and shifting about to hear. "So do the men who fought for us at Trenton and Monmouth and Long Island and Guilford Courthouse and Yorktown."

The men glanced at each other, not saying anything. Paul thought they looked ashamed.

Uncle Ethan stepped into the circle of workers. Father grinned. "Sorry to keep your men from their jobs, Ethan."

Uncle Ethan laughed, pushing back his long coat and stuffing his hands into the pockets of his buff-colored breeches. "You're never sorry to bend another man's ears with your ideas, Will, during the workday or not. It's almost five-thirty, about time for the men to quit anyway. They won't be able to see to work in a few minutes."

The men turned back to their work, collecting their tools and putting them in a shed where they'd be safe for the night.

"So this is where you've been stopping after school," Father said to Paul. "You shouldn't pester your uncle Ethan."

Paul's face grew hot. How could his father say such a thing right in front of Uncle Ethan!

"I like having Paul around," Uncle Ethan said. "He has a quick mind."

Uncle Ethan's praise took some of the sting out of Father's words, but not all of it. Why couldn't his father be more like

Uncle Ethan? Paul wondered. His uncle never said things that embarrassed him.

Father and Paul walked home together. Away from the open shipyard beside the harbor, the narrow, crooked streets lined with tall brick buildings seemed darker than ever. Shopkeepers were closing wooden shutters over their windows and carrying merchandise inside for the night.

Looking through house windows they passed, Paul could see housewives lighting evening candles and lanterns. Wood smoke from chimneys all over town blended with smells of meat and porridges and breads cooking. Paul's stomach growled at the mouthwatering odors.

All along the way, people greeted Father, welcoming him home and asking when he'd be returning to Washington's troops.

Once they moved to the edge of the street as a coach pulled by six bay horses passed. "That's John Hancock," Paul told Father.

"He was president of the First Continental Congress before the war started," Father said.

Paul told how he'd met Mr. Hancock when the famous man had ordered the broadsides about Cornwallis's surrender.

"One day you'll tell your grandchildren how you met one of the most important men in America," Father said.

Paul couldn't imagine ever being an old grandfather!

Mr. Hodgkins, a candlemaker who lived near them, joined them outside his shop. All the way home he and Father argued over what kind of government the United States should create now that the war was almost over.

Once they were home, Father and Paul hurried to the kitchen. Paul thought it was the best room in the house on a December evening like this. The huge stone fireplace that filled almost one entire wall kept the room toasty warm.

His mother had raked some hot coals from beneath the logs. At the edge of the hearth, a round, black Dutch oven sat over the coals. The Dutch oven was just a large kettle with legs and a cover. Paul could smell the cornbread cooking in the Dutch oven, though he couldn't see it. The Dutch oven cover was nearly hidden by more coals piled on top of it to keep the container hot enough to bake the bread.

Father wiped a smudge of ash from Mother's cheek and smiled. "Dinner about ready? Your men are home and hungry."

"It's almost ready. Rachel is dipping apple cider for everyone. Wash your hands, men."

Beside the back door stood a wooden bench with a wooden bucket of water on top of it. A wooden peg on the wall above the bucket held a small linen towel.

David was kneeling on the bench beside the bucket. Paul grinned as he walked across the kitchen. David must be sailing the small wooden boat Paul had whittled for him. He stopped beside the bucket and looked in. It wasn't David's toy boat in the bucket!

Paul grabbed a small, beautifully carved ship from the water. Unlike the simple toy he'd made for David, this ship looked like a real miniature ship, with every detail carved, and tiny ropes holding up linen sails. Uncle Ethan had given it to him, and it was his most treasured possession.

"Davey, I've told you never to play with this!"

David's face went from surprise to tears. He held out a pudgy hand. "Davey's toy!"

Paul shook his head hard. "No. Paul's toy. Don't touch."

Father poured water from the bucket into a chipped porcelain bowl on the bench. "Don't be selfish, Paul. Let him play with your toy."

Paul clutched the ship tighter. "But Father, Davey will break it."

Father picked up the tan square of soap that Mother had made from ashes and fat. "You're the oldest brother, Paul. You have to set a good example for the others."

"But. . ."

"Don't talk back."

Paul's eyes stung. He opened them wide to keep the tears that threatened from falling. Davey grabbed for the ship.

Mother caught Davey's hand in hers just in time. "Play with your own ship, Davey." She handed him the simple sailboat Paul had made for him. Davey's bottom lip jutted out.

Father stared at her. "I said he could play with Paul's ship."

"Paul's ship isn't a toy," Mother told him. "It's a fine carving. Davey knows he isn't allowed to play with it. Show it to your father, Paul."

Paul held out the ship. Father wiped his hands on the towel before taking it. He looked it over carefully, giving a low whistle. "This is fine. Where did you get it?"

"From Uncle Ethan."

Father frowned.

Now what had he done wrong? Paul wondered. A movement caught his attention. "Davey, what are you doing?"

"I'm goin' to sail on my ship."

Davey's little ship bobbed in the bucket. He'd climbed up on the bench and was just about to sit down on the floating ship.

"Don't, Davey!"

Too late!

Splash!

Water went everywhere. Davey's bottom stuck in the bucket. His arms and feet stuck straight in the air. Davey let out a yowl as loud as a cat with its tail slammed in a door. Paul and his parents burst out laughing. Davey wailed louder.

"Hold onto the bucket, Paul," Father instructed.

While Paul held the bucket's sides, Father grabbed Davey's hands and pulled him out. Water poured from his clothes. Father quickly removed them and hung them to dry in front of the fireplace. Then he took Davey upstairs for dry clothes while Paul mopped up the mess.

The mast on Davey's ship was broken, Paul saw, and the sail collapsed. He'd have to fix them after dinner. Then Paul put his own ship back on the painted mantle above the parlor fireplace. He kept it there because it was a high place Davey couldn't reach. He noticed his mother's best chair had been pulled close to the fireplace. Davey must have climbed on it to reach the ship. Paul pushed the chair back in place before going to dinner.

The hot cornbread smothered in maple syrup tasted good. When they'd finished their cornbread and baked apples, Father smiled at each one of them. "I have some news, and I want you all to be the first to hear it."

"What is it?" Paul asked.

"What? What?" Davey repeated, bouncing up and down in his chair. What and why were his two favorite words.

"I've decided not to reenlist in the army. I'm home for good."

Mother jumped up and threw her arms around his neck, but Paul just stared at him, then at Joel. Joel stared right back. He looked as unhappy with the news as Paul felt.

When Mother was seated again, Paul said, "I thought you said you were in the war at the beginning and you wanted to stay in the army until the end."

Father nodded. "So I did. But it looks like the Continentals won't be fighting for a while, at least in the North. If they do get into battle, I'll join up again. For now, I think I can do more important work for Massachusetts and the new United States at home in Boston."

"How?" Paul asked.

"How?" Davey echoed.

Father leaned forward, his forearms resting against the table. His brown eyes sparked with excitement. "I want to use the newspaper to convince the people we need money for the soldiers. They haven't been paid for a long time, and many are very poor. I want to print articles about the different ways the United States can choose to govern themselves, too. Until the states prove they can work together and run themselves well, the Revolution won't be over, no matter how many treaties are signed. We must ask God to guide us in forming our new government. You children can help."

"Us?" Paul asked, startled. "How?"

"How?" Davey repeated.

"You can pray. The Bible says, 'Except the Lord build the house, they labor in vain that build it.' We need His help building the house of our new country."

Father kept talking, but Paul didn't hear any more. He couldn't quite believe his father would be living with them after all these years. Paul shifted uncomfortably in his seat and studied his father's face. He wasn't sure he trusted his father's words. Would he truly stay, or would he change his mind and join the Continental army again in a few weeks, like he always had before?

CHAPTER 4
Meeting Lafayette

Maggie clumped down the wide stairway with the curving mahogany handrail, as ungraceful as always. Her green silk dress that matched her eyes had a wide skirt. Long lace swung at her elbows. A lacy white kerchief went around her shoulders and tucked into the top of her gown. Candlelight from brass wall sconces danced off her dainty gold chain and locket.

Her mother watched her from the bottom of the stairs with a scowl. "Maggie, for once, act like a proper young lady tonight.

Keep your back straight. Walk, stand, and sit gracefully. Don't forget to curtsy when introduced to your elders."

Shaking her head and clucking like a mother hen, Maggie's mother hurried into the parlor, leaving Maggie with her cousin Paul.

Maggie slumped onto the bottom step and dropped her chin into the palm of her hand. "I don't see why girls can't wear breeches like men. You can't run fast in a dress, and you always have to be careful you don't let it get too close to the fireplace."

Paul nodded, not really listening to her chatter. He was thinking that just once he'd like to slide down that long curving bannister! He looked through the open double doors into the drawing room. In his house it was much smaller and called a parlor. Uncle Ethan and Aunt Dancy's house was much grander than Paul's home. As a merchant and shipbuilder, Uncle Ethan made much more money than Paul's father. The rooms in the house were large with tall ceilings. The parlor walls were painted pale yellow, and blue velvet drapes hung at the windows.

As at Paul's house, some of the furniture had been in the family a long time. A great-great-grandfather had made it. Other furniture was new, like the small upholstered chairs with wood that was painted gold. Two oil paintings, one of Uncle Ethan and the other of Aunt Dancy, hung in oval frames over the fireplace.

The room was filled with candlelight. A candelabra hung from the ceiling in the middle of the room. Brass-backed candleholders hung on the walls. Tables and the mantle over the fireplace held candles with tall glass placed around them to prevent them from being accidently blown out by drafts.

The room smelled of burning candles, wood burning in the fireplace, and spices in the large silver bowl that held a warm punch.

Bright green holly and pine branches added color to the room.

Paul almost had to pinch himself to make sure he was truly there! Uncle Ethan had talked to Paul's father as promised. A neighbor was watching Rachel and Davey. Paul's only disappointment was that his younger brother Joel had come, too.

Paul's gaze rested on his black-haired brother. Joel stood between Father and Uncle Ethan beside the harpsichord. A sharp pain darted through Paul's chest. Would his father ever like him as much as he liked Joel?

His father and Joel spent lots of time together while Paul was at school. Paul was jealous of the time they spent together. His father never seemed to speak harshly to Joel, either.

"Isn't the harpsichord music beautiful?" Maggie asked. "Mother has promised I might have lessons."

"I didn't know you wanted to learn how to play."

She nodded, her eyes shining. "I've always wanted to, since I first heard one. When I begged for lessons years ago, Mother said we couldn't afford such luxuries during the war."

Paul looked at Maggie curiously. She looked very excited and happy. Did she want to play the harpsichord as much as he wanted to design ships? Did everyone have a secret wish inside them?

The grandfather clock at the top of the wide stairway bonged seven times. "When will your guests be here?" He'd barely finished the question when the door knocker sounded.

In a minute, Joel and Father joined Paul and Maggie. Father told the boys firmly that they mustn't pester the adults. Children had no place at a dinner party but to be introduced to the guests. Then they were to leave.

"Do you get to stay for the dinner party?" Paul asked Maggie.

"No. I can only stay until the guests sit down to eat."

It wasn't a large party. There were only about a dozen people invited, important people who Ethan thought Lafayette might enjoy visiting with, like Sam Adams. The whole town knew Mr. Adams didn't usually approve of extravagant parties, but this was different. It was only a small dinner, not a ball.

Father introduced each of the guests to Maggie and the boys.

The men were dressed in their best formal suits—some of velvet, others of satin in beautiful shades of green, violet, or blue. Vests were embroidered with silver, silver buttons glittered down the front of the coats, and silver buckles sparkled on their shoes.

Paul wore the suit he always wore for best in the winter, a maroon velvet. It was a bit worn on the bottom, but his long coat hid that. Joel's suit was dark blue. Neither of them had silver buttons or buckles.

The parlor was soon filled with the babble of people visiting, but Lafayette hadn't arrived.

Father allowed Maggie to bring some punch to the boys, who were seated on stiff, narrow chairs in the hallway. "How is the punch?"

"Good, sir." Paul looked down at the cup he held. He liked apple cider better.

Father wasn't dressed like most of the men. Instead he wore his uniform. Mother had worked and worked on it, cleaning it, pressing it, mending it. It would never look new again, but new uniforms cost money the family didn't have to spare. On one shoulder was a gold braid piece, called an epaulet, that told the world that Father was a captain in the Continental army. Father wouldn't be wearing the uniform much longer. He'd written a letter that day saying he wouldn't be returning to the army.

Moments later Lafayette arrived. The talking in the parlor quieted to a low murmur. Everyone studied the new guest, eager to see the famous man.

Paul watched as eagerly as everyone else. General Lafayette was tall, with sparkling eyes and a mouth that smiled quickly and often. His red hair was only slightly powdered. It was pulled straight back into a queue tied with a black ribbon.

"Isn't he charming?" Maggie whispered in his ear as Lafayette bent over a lady's hand.

Paul gave her a withering glance. Girls said the stupidest things! Maggie usually had better sense than most girls. "He's a great soldier, a leader and fighter."

"He's charming, too. What wonderful manners he has! Don't you love the way he talks?"

Paul rolled his eyes. "He talks like a French man speaking English, just like all the other French soldiers in town."

She wrinkled her nose at him.

Like Father, Lafayette wore his uniform, but it was in much better shape than Father's. It was a Continental uniform with off-white breeches and waistcoat and a blue jacket. He had huge epaulets on each shoulder. The gold buttons and braid on his jacket sparkled. Lace bobbed at his throat.

"He used his own money to buy uniforms for all the men in his regiment," Paul whispered to Joel.

Paul had been amazed when he first heard that. Every soldier had to pay for his own uniform. Most couldn't afford the Continental uniform and instead wore simple linen, leather, and wool clothes that would wear well in the backwoods and swamps.

"Is he rich?" Joel asked, his brown eyes wide.

"He must be. He came to America after he left military school and offered to fight for free."

"Why did he want to fight for us?"

"Because he loves liberty."

"But he doesn't even live in our country," Joel protested.

"He believes we're all brothers."

Joel frowned. "Like you and me?"

"No. Like. . ." Paul struggled to find the right words. "Like everyone is part of God's family, no matter what country they live in. He thinks we should all fight for each other's rights."

Lafayette was introduced to all the adults before Father brought him over to Maggie and the boys. Paul discovered with surprise that he'd been holding his breath in anticipation since he first saw the general headed toward them.

When Father introduced them, Paul bowed the way Uncle Ethan had taught him. Keeping his legs together and straight and his back straight, he bowed slightly from the waist. Lafayette bowed back, military fashion, with his hand on the hilt of his sword.

Joel tried to copy Paul's bow. Paul bit back a laugh when his brother bent too far and almost fell over.

Maggie curtsied to the general, like all the ladies had. When he took her hands and touched his lips to her fingers in the way she'd thought so charming, Paul heard her draw a startled gasp. Her cheeks grew as pink as if she'd been sitting too close to the fireplace's heat.

"Margaret is a true patriot," Father told Lafayette. "When she heard the soldiers needed more winter clothing, she decided to do something about it. She convinced her girlfriends to come to her house every morning. They worked together spinning wool and knitting mittens for the Continentals. We call the girls Maggie's Soldiers."

Maggie bit her lips. Paul could see she was both pleased and embarrassed.

Lafayette grinned. "Ah, she is a soldier indeed, with needles and a spinning wheel for weapons instead of a musket and bayonet.

I assure you, cherie, you are the army's most beautiful soldier."

Maggie smiled. Her cheeks grew redder. "I wish I were a boy, so I could have truly joined the Continentals!"

Joel chuckled. Paul bit his lips to keep from laughing, too.

The general's eyes widened for a moment at Maggie's bold statement, but he only said, "It is the army's loss. I'm sure you would have been one of Washington's best soldiers." Then he shrugged, and the epaulets on his shoulder rose and fell. "But then, who would have made the mittens for the soldiers, mon cherie?"

She giggled, then sobered. "My brother Charles fought."

"This makes you sad? Was he killed? Injured?"

Her curls danced when she shook her head. "He's a prisoner of war, in a prison ship off Long Island."

Lafayette rested a hand on her shoulder. "He has given a great deal for your new country. When the peace treaty is signed, he will come home to you."

Maggie smiled and nodded.

"And the boys, Captain Lankford, they are yours?" the general asked, turning his gaze on Paul and Joel.

Paul felt suddenly shy.

"Yes. Paul is the oldest. He's eight," Father said. "My wife says she doesn't know what she would have done without him while I've been away. He's been a great help to her with the printing shop."

"Ah, yes. The newspaper. Then this must be the son you mentioned to me at Yorktown, mon ami."

Paul's gaze jerked to his father. He hadn't told them he'd met Lafayette before!

Lafayette smiled down. "There was an English drummer boy at Yorktown, a brave lad. Your father said you had a heart as large and full of courage as that boy's."

His father had said that? Paul couldn't think of a reply.

Lafayette turned toward Joel.

"Sir!" Paul started.

The general turned back, raised eyebrows questioning.

"I. . .I wanted to thank you, sir," Paul stammered. "For helping us. For fighting with us and convincing the rest of France to fight with us."

"For liberty!" Joel interrupted.

The general smiled at Joel. "For all men's liberty. Now the war is all but over. It will be your turn to fight to keep the dearly bought liberty."

Paul blinked. "You mean, we'll have to go to war?"

"Not the way you mean, not as soldiers with muskets and cannons." Lafayette shook his head soberly. "No, your fight will be keeping your liberty through the choices you and your fellow Americans make every day."

Paul didn't understand. He could see by Joel's frown that he didn't understand, either.

Lafayette leaned down, put a hand on each boy's shoulder, and said in a loud whisper, "I'd rather slide down that bannister than visit with everyone in the drawing room, wouldn't you?"

Paul grinned, imagining the famous major general sliding the bannister in his elegant uniform just as Paul dreamed of doing himself!

When Lafayette joined the other adults, Paul asked, "Why didn't you tell us you knew him, Father?"

"I don't know him well. Many of the officers who fought together have at least spoken to each other."

"Is he as great as people say?" Paul asked.

Father rested a hand on Paul's shoulder, but his gaze followed the tall, redheaded general. "He's as great a man as I've ever known. He could have been at General Washington's side at Cornwallis's surrender. Before Yorktown, Lafayette was second in command to Washington. Lafayette volunteered to step down to another position so General Lincoln would be second in command at the surrender."

"Who is General Lincoln?" Joel asked.

"Cornwallis's sword was surrendered to General Lincoln," Paul answered quietly.

"Yes." His father nodded. "Now, you two must get home. See you don't dally along the way. Maggie, will you get them a lantern, please?"

When she handed them the lit lantern at the door, she whispered, "You see? General Lafayette is charming!"

Paul and Joel just laughed.

The boys didn't dally. It was too chilly out to walk slowly. Paul glanced up at the streetlight they passed. It would be nice on a dark night like this to have streetlights. He couldn't remember ever seeing them lit. His mother said they hadn't been lit since before the war. The town hadn't money to spend on oil for streetlights. The streets looked different at night, with only a few lanterns to light the shadows.

His father seemed different tonight, too. Why did he admire Lafayette for giving up his position instead of for being a good army leader and bringing France to help them fight? His father had been in the army almost all Paul's life. He'd thought his father admired brave soldiers more than anyone else.

"Can I carry the lantern?" Joel asked.

Paul gave it to him. He was sure Joel wanted it because the little heat it gave off would help warm his hands. Paul didn't mind. He stuffed his hands beneath his cloak.

In the silence of his thoughts, Paul examined the most important thing he'd heard all night: His father had told the great General Lafayette that his son had a heart full of courage. Did he truly think that? The thought warmed him all the way home.

CHAPTER 5
Fights in the Family

"Is that ink ready yet?" Father asked.

"Almost, sir," Paul replied.

Paul poured lampblack into a large old kettle. Picking up a wooden paddle, he stirred the lampblack into the rosin and linseed oil already in the kettle. His mother had told him that before the war, England had made the American colonies buy all their ink from England. During the war, they couldn't buy it from England, so Mother had learned to make it herself.

Paul thought it was a lot of work, especially when his brothers and sister were outside playing! But he stirred faithfully, while his parents studied the written copies of the articles they'd be printing that evening.

"Father, the ink is ready."

"Good." Father patted Paul's shoulder. "You're a fine help about the shop. Run and find your brothers, so we can have a bit of dinner before we begin printing the newspaper. See you don't stop by the wharves or shipyard on the way home."

Paul hurried out the door and onto the cobblestone street before Father could change his mind. He dashed down the street, the breeze he created rushing through his hair in a way that always made him feel completely free and powerful.

He hated being cooped up in the dark, gloomy print shop. At the shipyard, men worked in the fresh air and sunshine. He hardly ever got to go to the shipyard anymore. His father always found work for Paul to do around the print shop after school let out at five: carrying and cutting paper, delivering papers, helping to dampen paper and hang the papers up to dry when Father and James ran the press, or mixing ink.

Now that May was here and there were hours of sunshine after school, Paul especially hated working at the shop. May, Paul thought. His father had been home for six months. It looked like he was home to stay this time after all.

He raced through the low early grass and weeds to a small pond. Joel, Davey, Rachel, and Maggie were all there. Davey and Rachel, as usual, were sailing their toy ships near a large rock at the pond's edge. Joel and Maggie were on a raft a few feet offshore.

"Hey, where'd you get the raft?" Paul called, running out onto the flat rock where Davey and Rachel knelt.

"We found it in the bushes over there!" Joel pointed at a clump of scratchy gooseberry bushes at the far end of the pond.

Maggie and Joel used the long branches they held as poles and pushed the raft to shore. Paul helped them drag it up on land.

"I wanted to be General Rochambeau, but Maggie said she got to be him," Joel complained.

Maggie wrinkled her nose at him. "I can be whoever I want to be, 'cause I'm oldest."

"She tried to make me be Benedict Arnold," Joel told Paul.

"You should have told her you were John Paul Jones," Paul said. "He won a great naval battle for us in the war."

He looked over the raft. It was only a bunch of logs tied together with leather strips.

"Do you think we could put a sail on it?" Joel asked eagerly.

"Then we could really sail!" Maggie agreed.

"We could, but I could make a better one with leftover timber from the shipyard." Paul pointed to the bottom of one of the logs. "See how rotten that log is? And the leather strips don't hold the logs together too well."

"We could ask Father to build one," Maggie said.

Paul just grunted. It would be a lot more fun to build it themselves. He was sure he could do it, if Uncle Ethan let him use scraps and tools from the shipyard.

"Maggie's right. We should ask Uncle Ethan," Joel agreed. "You don't have time to build one. You're always at school."

It seemed to Paul that Joel was right. He was either at school or helping at the shop. "Soon you'll be seven, and then you'll go to school, too." Paul stood up, wiping his damp hands on his breeches.

"What are you doin' with my raft?" a voice called.

Paul spun around. At the sight of the angry, red-haired boy, Paul groaned.

"Who is it?" Joel asked.

"Andrew. He's two years older than me. He's the worst bully in our school."

Andrew marched up to Paul, planted a freckled hand on Paul's shoulder, and shoved him. "Who said you could use my raft?"

Anger surged through Paul, but he knew better than to shove Andrew back. He'd seen Andrew beat other kids up, always kids like Paul who were smaller and younger than Andrew. "We didn't know it was your raft. Sorry."

"Sorry isn't good enough." Andrew shoved him again.

"Stop that," Maggie demanded.

Andrew's lip curled up in a sneer. "You let girls fight for you now, Paul?"

Oh, no, Paul thought. *I'll never hear the end of this.* "I can take care of myself, Maggie."

"Why are you picking a fight with Paul, Andrew?" Maggie demanded hotly. "He didn't use your stupid raft. Joel and I did."

"Oh?" Andrew turned to her. "So I should be teaching you a lesson, instead." He gave her a shove, and she stumbled backward.

Maggie was older than Paul, but no bigger. *Besides, she's a girl. She doesn't know how to fight,* Paul thought.

Paul moved next to Maggie. "If you touch her again, you'll have to fight me, too."

Joel stepped beside Paul and stuck out his chin. "Me, too."

Andrew took a step back, shaking his head. "You three little kids aren't worth fighting."

He pushed his raft back into the pond and grabbed a pole. A

minute later, he and the raft were moving across the water.

Davey and Rachel, who had been watching from the water's edge, knelt down to play with their boats again.

"He would have fought if there weren't three of us, wouldn't he?" Maggie asked.

Paul nodded. "He's beaten up lots of kids. I've never seen him beat up a girl, though."

Davey tugged at Paul's breeches. "Look, Paul! My ship has a captain!"

Davey's ship bobbed beside shore. A baby turtle rested on top of it.

Paul grinned. "It sure does, Davey. Are you going to take the turtle home?"

Davey nodded.

Their mother was used to Paul and Joel bringing little animals home with them. This was the first time Davey had, though, except for the insects he always stuffed into the tops of his knee-high stockings last summer.

"What are you going to call him?" Paul asked.

"Captain."

"That's a good name. I think he's sailing your ship a bit far from shore, though." Paul knelt and reached for the ship. It was just beyond arm's length. He scooped at the water, creating a wave that carried it in close enough for him to reach. He grabbed the turtle first, before it could slide off into the water, and then grabbed the boat.

"It's time to go home for dinner," he said, handing the turtle and ship to Davey.

Joel dropped down at the water's edge where Rachel was still sailing her own ship. "I want to play longer."

"Me, too." Davey squatted down beside him.

Paul settled his fists on his hips. "You can't. We have to go home now."

Joel looked over his shoulder and stuck out his tongue. "You aren't our father. You can't tell us what to do."

"You're not Father," Davey repeated.

A few minutes ago, Joel had stood up to Andrew with Paul. Now he was acting like they were enemies. Anger boiled through Paul. He clenched his fists and glared at Joel's back. For years, Joel, Rachel, and Davey had done as Paul said. It had been Paul's responsibility to watch out for them. Now Joel sassed him whenever he gave him an order, and Davey was beginning to copy him.

"Father sent me to tell you to come home now," Paul yelled.

Rachel stood up with her dripping boat. "I'll come."

Joel and Davey ignored him.

"If you stay, you'll be in trouble with Father," Paul warned. He plucked Davey's ship and turtle from the water. "Come on, Davey."

Davey shook his head and tried to take the ship and turtle back.

"You're hungry, aren't you, Davey?" Maggie asked.

Davey shook his head no and pressed his lips together hard. He tried to pry Paul's fingers from the ship.

"Won't it be fun to show Father your turtle, Davey?"

Davey's face broke into a grin.

"Hold out your hands," Paul commanded. Davey held them out together, palms up. Paul put the little turtle into them. Immediately Captain tried to crawl over the edge.

"No! Captain, no!" Davey yelled, not knowing how to stop it.

Paul caught Captain before it could fall. Then he showed Davey how to let the turtle sit in one palm while Davey held the fingers of his other hand loosely around the turtle so it couldn't crawl away. Captain looked at all the fingers and tucked its head inside its shell. Davey giggled.

It took longer than usual to walk home. Davey walked slowly, holding his hands carefully in the way Paul had showed him so Captain wouldn't fall.

Joel walked home by himself, a ways behind the others. Paul knew he was trying to show that he didn't have to do what Paul said, even though Paul was the oldest.

As soon as they reached home, Paul knew he was in trouble.

"Where have you been?" Father scolded. "You didn't stop at the shipyard did you? Didn't I tell you to come right home?"

Paul burned with anger inside. Why did his father blame him? He hadn't even asked why they were late.

But when Davey held out Captain for Father to see, Father asked if he could hold Captain and told Davey what a great turtle he was. "He can sail a ship," Davey told him eagerly.

Paul hid a laugh behind his hand. He saw his father trying not to laugh, too.

Father offered to help Davey find a crock to keep the turtle in. Davey agreed. When they found the crock, Father said, "We'd best go outside and get a rock for Captain. He'll need a place to rest out of the water." He held out his hand to Davey.

Davey stared at his hand a minute, then turned and ran across the room to grab Paul's hand in both his own. He dropped his head back and leaned against Paul. "Will you help me find a rock?"

"Sure," Paul said. "Let's ask Father to watch Captain for you while we look."

Davey turned around, his brown eyes wide. "Will you watch Captain, Father?"

Paul could see the disappointment in his father's face, but Father smiled and agreed to watch the turtle.

Now that their father had been home for six months, Joel and Rachel seemed to like Father a lot more than they did Paul. Before they always looked up to Paul. Now he was just another kid. Only Davey still trusted Paul more than their father. Paul had been trying to get Davey to trust their father more.

But part of me is glad Davey likes me best, he thought while he and Davey picked over the stones at the side of the street.

When they went back inside, Father and Mother were arguing over an article they would be printing that night. Paul remembered the article was about a rumor that made his father mad. Some Continental army officers suggested the new states combine into one country and make George Washington their king. Many people liked the idea. Washington had proven he was a wise leader. But General Washington was very angry at the suggestion. He didn't think the United States should have a king. Paul guessed he must feel like Father.

"One of the reasons the war was fought," his father had said, "was to make sure people in America could always choose their leaders and the people who made their laws. Kings have too much power. The only king we want in America is King Jesus!"

But now Mother and Father were arguing over the way the article should be laid out in the newspaper. It wasn't the first time they'd disagreed about the paper since Father had come back. Paul hated when they argued. It made his stomach feel weird.

Father won this argument. He always did. Mother set her lips firmly together. She spun about, the skirts of her long old work dress and apron whirling, and stalked into the kitchen.

Paul followed. She was filling wooden bowls with thick, golden pumpkin soup from the kettle hanging on the crane over the fireplace. The soup smelled of the onion and spices she'd added to it. Paul sat down on the high-backed wooden settle beside the fireplace and offered to hold the bowls while his mother filled them. She thanked him with a smile and handed him a bowl. Paul watched her fill it. He didn't know quite what to say to her.

Before his father came home, his mother talked about the business and home matters with Paul. She didn't always do things the way Paul wished, but she always asked his opinion. Now she talked everything over with his father instead. They made the decisions and then told Paul and the other children what they were to do.

It's like the adults have their own secret world, Paul thought, *and children can't enter, no matter what.*

Still, he didn't like the way his father treated his mother, arguing with her like that. He took a deep breath and told himself not to feel scared.

"Mother, why doesn't Father listen to you about the newspaper? You ran it for six years while he was away. You know a lot about newspapers."

She smiled and tweaked his hair. "I think so, too, but it's your father's newspaper. It belonged to his father. He has a right to run it as he wishes."

Paul wasn't sure that was a good answer. "Doesn't he care that it upsets you when he insists on doing things his way?"

Mother took the last bowl from his hands and set it down on the worktable in the middle of the room. Then she sat beside him on the settle and took his hands in hers.

"Whenever I get mad at your father, I remember that I prayed for six years that God would bring him back safe from the war and let us live together like a normal family again. When I remember all those years and all those prayers, getting my own way isn't important anymore."

Paul thought he understood what she was saying. He was glad God had kept his father safe during the war, too. But why had God's answer to their prayers made life harder for the family instead of easier?

CHAPTER 6

The Secret in the Attic

That night, something woke Paul. He sat up and rubbed his eyes.

"Squeak! Squeak!"

He froze. What was that?

Moonlight shone in through the window, but he couldn't see much in its dim light. Beside him, Joel slept soundly. Maybe he had just imagined the noise, or dreamt it.

Something scampered across his legs. Paul yanked his legs to his chest. A moment later a thin black shadow squiggled across the bottom of the bed. Prickles ran over Paul's scalp. He jumped up, trying to keep his balance on the soft feather bed, and watched the slithering shadow. He opened his mouth to scream, but the sound stuck in his throat.

"Mmmmm." Joel moved under the blankets. "What're you doin'?"

"A. . .a. . .a snake! It's a snake!"

Joel sat up. "What?"

Paul pointed at the shadow sliding off the end of the bed. "Look!" His finger trembled, but so did the rest of him!

Their bedroom door flew open. Their father and mother raced in, their nightcaps flying. Father wore only his long linen shirt and Mother the linen gown she wore under her work clothes during the day.

"What's the trouble?" Father demanded.

Paul pointed again at the end of the bed. "A snake! There's a snake in our room!"

Joel scurried out of bed. "Don't hurt it! It's my pet!"

"Your pet?" Father stared at him, hands on his hips.

"Your pet?" Paul repeated. "You can't keep a snake in our bedchamber!"

Joel dropped to the floor and looked under the bed. "We have to find it. It's probably chasing my mouse."

"Your mouse?" Mother's voice was almost as high and squeaky as a mouse's. She lifted her skirt and glanced fearfully around the floor.

Father picked up the tinderbox on the bedside table. As usual, it took a few tries to get a light. A minute later he had a candle lit.

"When did you get a snake and mouse?" Paul asked Joel.

"Why didn't you tell me you had them?"

"Why didn't you tell me?" their mother asked.

Joel's black curls peeked over the end of the bed. "Will you help me catch my snake before he eats my mouse?"

"Joel's right," Father agreed crisply. "Time for explanations later." He knelt down and set the candle on the floor so it would shine beneath the bed.

"Tell me when it's over." Mother left, closing the door behind her so the snake and mouse couldn't sneak into another part of the house.

Paul was embarrassed that everyone had seen him jumping around, screaming about the snake. He wasn't afraid of snakes that weren't poisonous. Still, he didn't like being surprised by them, like when they wiggled over his toes in tall grass beside a pond. And he certainly didn't expect snakes in his bed!

He climbed down and knelt beside his father. "Can't you see him?"

"Not yet."

Paul cautiously laid the side of his head against the wooden floor and studied the bottom of the low bed. The snake had to be there. There weren't many other places in the room it could hide. "There it is!"

"Where?" Father and Joel asked at the same time. Their bottoms went up in the air and their cheeks to the floor as they looked where Paul was looking.

Paul pointed. "Right there, wrapped around that rope." Sure enough, the snake was wrapped about one of the ropes pulled across the bottom of the bed.

"It's your snake, Joel," Father said. "You get it unwound."

Joel crawled under the bed on his back. There was barely room for him. It took him a few minutes to find the snake.

"Where were you keeping it?" Paul asked.

"In your tin lunch pail."

"Yuk!" Paul scrunched his face together. What a surprise he might have had for his next lunch!

"You'd better put him back there while we look for the mouse," Father said.

"How did he get out?" Paul asked.

"I left the cover open, just a crack," Joel explained, "so he could breathe."

"Didn't you know he would crawl out? Why didn't you tie a piece of paper over it and poke holes in it, like Mother taught us?"

"I didn't want Mother to see him. I knew she wouldn't let me keep him."

"You're right about that." Father chuckled. "Better put him back in the pail with the cover tight this time and help me look for that mouse."

There wasn't much furniture for even something as small as a mouse to hide behind, but they couldn't find it. At least they knew the snake hadn't eaten the mouse. They gave up looking.

Father ordered Joel to take the snake outside and let it go. "And I don't want to see another snake brought into this house. Is that clear?"

"Yes, sir," Joel mumbled. His shoulders drooped beneath the linen shirt that reached almost to his knees.

Paul chuckled.

His father scowled down at him. "I don't want you encouraging him. You're the oldest. You need to set a good example."

Paul stared at him in surprise. "I didn't do anything. I didn't even know he had the snake and mouse."

"Acting like it's funny won't help him learn to do the right thing."

"No, sir." Paul stared after his father as he left the room. Resentment boiled in his chest. His father made it sound like it was Paul's fault Joel brought home the snake and mouse!

He crawled into the soft bed to wait for Joel. He wished his father had never come home from the war!

The next day after school, Paul studied the large drawing of a ship lying on Uncle Ethan's desk in his office. Each piece of the ship in the drawing had a number beside it, telling how long and wide it would be when built. More of this ship would ride beneath the water than on top of it.

"How do you know how high to make the main mast?" Paul asked. The main mast was the tallest and held the largest sails.

"It's all mathematical," Uncle Ethan answered. "Multiply the width of the ship by twelve and divide that number by five. For every three feet in height, the mast must be one inch thick."

Paul grinned. "I guess I'd better study arithmetic hard in school if I want to build ships."

"Do you remember the best wood to use for masts?"

"Pine," Paul answered promptly, "because it's straighter and lighter than other wood."

Uncle Ethan had given Paul a sketchbook with a soft leather cover so he could practice drawing ships. Paul shook his head as he studied Uncle Ethan's drawing. "My drawings will never be as good as yours."

"One day yours will be better than mine."

Paul's heart glowed from the compliment. "Do you truly think so?"

"I do. Everything is hard when it's new. You already draw better than I did at your age. You have a heart for designing ships, Paul. It's a wonderful gift when God puts a desire in a person's heart to do something special."

Paul played with a corner of the paper. "My father thinks I'm lazy because I'd rather be here than at the print shop."

There was a long moment when neither of them said anything. The only sounds came from the shipyard and wharves below, where men worked and gulls cried.

"Has your father told you to stay away from here?"

Paul shook his head. "No, only not to come too often. He's always telling me I should be more interested in politics and how the country is run. He says I waste my time coming down here. He wants me to be a printer when I grow up."

Paul tried to like his father, but it was so hard. They were so different. Paul always told Uncle Ethan everything, but he didn't dare tell him that he didn't know how to love his father. If he knew, Uncle Ethan might think Paul was awful and not be his friend anymore.

"Did you know Benjamin Franklin worked in his brother's printing office when he was a boy?" Uncle Ethan asked.

"He did?"

"Right here in Boston. He didn't like working there, so he ran away." Uncle Ethan grinned. "I hope you won't run away. It would be better to tell your father how you feel."

"Do. . .do you think you might tell him I'd rather build ships than be a printer?"

"That is something you must tell him yourself."

Paul didn't say anything. He knew he didn't have the courage to tell his father.

Uncle Ethan looked out the window overlooking the shipyard. "Ben Franklin will be in Paris soon. The peace talks will begin before long, and Mr. Franklin will be there to make decisions for our country. Being a printer is a good thing, but God had something different in mind for Mr. Franklin, didn't He?"

Paul stayed at the shipyard with Uncle Ethan as long as he dared. When he arrived home, his father was already home from the shop. "Where have you been? School let out hours ago."

"I was at Uncle Ethan's shipyard."

"You spend so much time down by the harbor that you could just as well be a wharf rat."

His father's words hurt so badly that Paul didn't even try to think of an answer. He opened his eyes wide to keep the tears from falling. He didn't want his father to know how much he hurt. His father wouldn't care anyway, he thought. He went into the kitchen to see if he could help his mother.

"Would you sift some flour for me?" She handed him the round wooden sieve.

Paul used a mug to dip flour from the barrel and put it into the sieve. The sieve was made of long strings from the tail of a horse woven across the space between the round wooden sides. He sifted the sieve back and forth above a large wooden bowl. Brown flour poured through the horse hairs. Anything else in the flour was caught in the sieve.

His mother looked over his shoulder. "Look at the mouse droppings in that sieve! And your brother thought we needed another mouse in the house!"

Paul grinned. They still hadn't found Joel's field mouse. Had it left the droppings in the flour? Probably not. There were always mice in the cellar, where they stored vegetables, fruit, and flour. Because of the mouse droppings and bugs, Mother always had to sift the flour before they could use it.

When dinner was over, the family gathered as usual in the parlor. Usually their father had Paul and Joel read aloud from the Bible each night to practice their reading or copy passages from it to practice writing. Tonight he had a newspaper from New York they read instead. Their mother's small spinning wheel buzzed and clicked while she worked beside the fire.

Every time Paul looked at his father, he remembered his words: wharf rat. As soon as he could get away from the rest of the family, he hurried upstairs. Soon he heard Joel's footsteps on the stairs. He wanted to be alone tonight. Where could he go? The attic!

Paul took the tinderbox and candle from the bedside table and slipped up the narrow attic steps. The roof sloped steeply above him when he reached the attic. The candle didn't give much light in such a large, dark space. He had to be careful to watch where he walked so he didn't trip over anything or bump his head on the ceiling beams.

He sat down beside a round-topped trunk, slumping against it. The floor and trunk were awful hard. He looked about for something soft to sit on.

Something stirred on the other side of the trunk. Paul lifted the candle and looked closer. A tiny brown-gray face beneath huge ears stared back. A field mouse!

"How did you get up here? Were you looking for a place to be alone, too?" Paul supposed he should try to catch the mouse, but he felt sorry for it. Besides, it hadn't asked to be brought into the house.

"Seen a blanket?" he asked the little creature. Then he opened the trunk. Maybe there'd be a blanket in it. There wasn't. Instead it was filled with things his father had brought back from the war. His uniform, the Bible he'd carried, his mess kit, the tattered, two-cornered hat, and some cartridge papers.

Paul looked through everything, curious. The last thing he found was a small, worn, brown leather book. The corners were bent. The leather looked like someone had beat it and left it out in the rain. Gold letters that were almost scratched off said "Journal."

Paul picked it up, started to open it, and put it back. It was like snooping to read what someone else had written. But he couldn't stop wondering what was in that book.

He could ask his father if he could read it. "He might say no," he told the mouse. "But he wrote letters home about the war for Mother to print in the newspaper. He couldn't have any secrets, could he?"

Ignoring his prickling conscience, Paul opened the book.

CHAPTER 7
Another Side to Father

"April 19, 1775," Paul read. That was the date of the battles of Lexington and Concord, the battles that started the war.

The first part of the entry told the story of the battles. Paul had heard it many times how Paul Revere and other riders had let the countryside know that the redcoats were coming to take the colonists' ammunition and cannons at Concord; how no one knew who started the battle at Lexington, but the first Patriots had been killed there; how the battle started again at Concord; how the redcoats marched down the road from Concord to Lexington to Charlestown, bright red targets for the Patriots who fired from behind houses, bushes, stone fences, and trees along the way.

"War is here at last. We must fight for our beliefs and prove to the world we will not lose this battle for every man's rights.

"War cannot be God's first choice. Yet what else are we to do when all other efforts have failed, when the king continues to take away citizens' rights? May God go before us. May our battle be His battle. May His blessing rest on our efforts.

"To offer my own life for such a great cause is a small matter. But Eliza and Paul, what of them?"

Paul caught his breath at the words, reread them, and continued on.

"Can it be right, as much as I believe in the Patriots' cause, to leave them? What if I'm killed or hurt and can no longer provide for them?

"I try to comfort myself with Eliza's words the morning I left Boston. She agreed I had to do what I believe in my heart is right, that if God meant for me to fight, God would watch over her and Paul while I was away."

Paul stared at the words. He'd thought his father hadn't cared about his family all the years he'd been in the army, but he had.

Thank You, Lord, he whispered into the dark.

Paul thought the summer went by way too quickly. He spent as many hours after school at the shipyard and wharves as he could. He wished school didn't last six days a week all year long! And he wished his father would stop calling him a wharf rat!

He fell into bed so tired every night that he forgot all about the journal.

Joel started school that summer, so he no longer spent time playing or with their father while Paul studied.

Andrew started bullying Joel, just like he'd always done to Paul. "When we're bigger, he won't dare pick on us anymore," Paul told Joel.

"Maybe we'll beat him up then," Joel said.

Andrew and his friends still played with the raft on the pond. Paul, Joel, and Maggie talked more about building a raft of their own.

"I don't think we should ask Uncle Ethan to build it," Paul said.

"Why not?" Maggie asked. "My father would make a good one."

"He might not let us build one at all. He might think it's dangerous for us to play on rafts."

"Father might not like it, either," Joel said. "Maybe he wouldn't let us play at the pond anymore if he found out about the raft."

"I suppose it is dangerous," Maggie agreed with a long face. "We probably shouldn't make one for ourselves."

Paul's conscience told him she was right. "But it would be a lot of fun to have one, wouldn't it? We could play pirates, or war, or Christopher Columbus finding America, or all kinds of things."

Maggie grinned. "We'd be careful."

"Can you build a raft for us, Paul?" Joel asked.

"I can do it." Paul ignored his conscience. "It won't be as good as I'd like it to be, since we can't ask Uncle Ethan for all the things I'd like to use."

"I bet it'll be better than that old Andrew's, anyway," Maggie said.

Paul did ask Uncle Ethan if he could use some scrap lumber.

"Of course. What are you planning to build?" his uncle asked.

"Oh, I just want to play with it," Paul said. He didn't want to lie to Uncle Ethan, but he didn't want to tell him the whole truth, either.

"This raft is much better than Andrew's," Joel told him when it was finished.

"I knew it would be," Maggie agreed.

Their praise made Paul feel ten feet high.

They had lots of fun with the raft. But when Andrew and his friends challenged them to a race, they lost, in spite of having a better raft. After the race, they watched Andrew and his friends walk away laughing.

"We didn't lose because of your raft," Joel assured Paul. "We lost because they're all bigger and stronger than we are."

Paul knew his brother was right, but it didn't make him feel better about losing. He wanted to beat Andrew in the worst way.

One fall evening after school, Paul and Joel met Maggie as they passed through North Square. It was busy with farmers loading into two-wheeled carts what vegetables, chickens, geese, and hogs they hadn't sold that day. Smells and noise of protesting animals mixed with the usual city smells, but the boys barely noticed. The market was always that way.

Maggie had a market basket over her arm, covered with a blue-and-white-striped linen cloth. "The post rider brought letters from Uncle Cuyler. I was going to take the letter to your house when I was done with the marketing, but you can take it."

"What did Uncle Cuyler say?" Joel asked.

"He said that the Loyalists in New York are worried about what they'll do when the treaty is signed and the redcoats leave," Maggie said. "There won't be anyone to protect them. Thousands of Loyalists fought with the redcoats against the Patriots. Of course, no one wants them living in America anymore."

"Maybe they can go back to England," Paul suggested.

Maggie shrugged. "Uncle Cuyler says most of the Loyalists can't afford to go anywhere. Many of them had to leave their homes and land and most of their possessions when the war broke out. General Howe, the redcoat leader in New York, has written to the king to ask England to help the Loyalists."

It might be a long time before they had an answer from the king, Paul thought. In good weather, it took a ship five or six weeks to cross the ocean to England. When the king received the letter, he'd have to decide what to do. The trip back to America would take another five or six weeks, if the weather didn't turn bad. With winter coming, it might take longer. In the winter there were often bad storms that delayed ships on the ocean.

When Paul and Joel reached the print shop, they were surprised to find James there alone, cleaning up after the day's work. Damp handbills hung from the poles by the ceiling. Father had already gone home.

Paul and Joel ran all the way to the house. If their father had already left the shop, he would be sure to scold them for coming home late! They hurried inside. Voices were coming from the kitchen, so they headed that way. They were almost to the kitchen door when they heard Father say, "I didn't want the boys to hear this. I thought it might frighten them."

Paul and Joel stopped, staring at each other. They stepped softly to the wall beside the door, where they could hear but not be seen.

"What might frighten them?" their mother was asking.

"Remember the letter Ben Franklin sent a couple months ago? He said that the king was less willing to grant the American colonies independence than he was earlier."

"Yes."

"Henry Knox has written me. General Washington thinks we should stop preparing for peace and instead prepare to continue the war. I. . .I'm thinking of reenlisting in the army."

Paul and Joel didn't let on that they'd heard their parents talking, not even when Father asked at the dinner table if the cat had their tongues.

Later that evening, Paul stole up the attic steps with his candle. He wanted to be alone and just think, without Joel or Davey or Rachel pestering him.

He brought some corn kernels with him for the mouse. They'd become quite friendly. The mouse often sat on the opposite end of the trunk from him, just watching him. Sometimes Paul talked things over with him.

He placed the kernels on the trunk, then settled down beside the trunk and thought about his father's words. Fear and sadness filled him. Why did he feel so strange? He'd wished a hundred times that his father would go back to the army. He'd been unhappy about so many things since his father came home. So why didn't he want him to go back to the army now?

Paul gave up trying to figure it out and pulled out his father's journal. For a minute he stared at the tattered, dirt-stained cover, rubbing his fingers over the letters. Would his father take it with him if he went back to the army? Would he have more battles to write about?

After the battles of Lexington and Concord, the British had retreated to Boston. The American soldiers gathered at Bunker Hill on Charlestown peninsula across the Charles River from Boston. Three months after Lexington, there was the battle of Bunker Hill.

"We watched the British soldiers, two thousand of them, come across the Charles River," his father wrote.

"We hadn't much ammunition, and our officers gave orders to waste no shot. Father was beside me when the first line of redcoats stormed us. I saw sweat break out on his upper lip as we waited. Nothing in my life was ever so hard as waiting for the redcoats to get close. The enemy's shots rang about our ears, and still we held our fire.

"A couple of our men took shots. Our officers ran along the top of the embankment we hid behind, braving the redcoats' musket shots. They picked up rifles, ordering us not to shoot until we could not possibly miss.

"I thought the order to fire would never come. Sweat was running into my eyes when I finally heard it. Most of the redcoats' front line fell when we fired. Almost all their officers were killed or wounded. The rest of the redcoats ran back to the beach.

"We jumped up with victory yells on our lips, ready to follow. Our officers ordered us to wait. The redcoats regrouped and came at us again. I felt sorry for them, climbing over their dead and wounded comrades to reach us.

"It was easier to wait for the order to fire this time. I could almost see the fear in the redcoats' eyes by the time we heard the fire order. Again, the redcoats' line was destroyed, and those escaping retreated to the beach to regroup.

"Many were climbing back into their boats, and I hoped fervently they would give up the fight and return to Boston, for many of our men were already out of ammunition. But the few remaining redcoats' officers would not allow them to run from poorly trained Patriots. Again the redcoats headed toward us. This time, there were only a few shots from our lines to slow them down.

"Smoke rolled over the hill from behind us, making it difficult to see the enemy. Later we discovered the redcoats had set Charlestown on fire. The entire city burned.

"My ammunition ran out, and I saw Father's had also. No one close to us had any ammunition left, and still our officers did not sound retreat. Now I wonder that I didn't feel more fear. Perhaps I hadn't time to realize our utter helplessness except for God.

"The redcoats charged us with bayonets. Of course, we had no bayonets. We swung our musket barrels at them, threw stones at them, anything we could get our hands on became weapons!

"Foot by foot the redcoats forced us back until they won Bunker Hill from us. Father was shot in his leg. With his arm about my neck, I helped him back from the fighting.

"It was a glorious day. Though we lost the hill and the battle, only 150 of our men were killed, 270 wounded. We hear that the British had more than 200 killed and more than 800 wounded.

"It was a horrible day. To see men fight for their lives with musket butts and stones against shooting muskets and bayonets. To see brave men friends, neighbors die because they believe in liberty. To see a city burned to the ground by our king's troops. To see a hill covered in dead and wounded men, with blood everywhere. To hear the screams of the wounded and dying.

"It seems a small thing to risk my own life to keep the rights Englishmen have known for centuries. But to watch friends die horrible deaths for my rights, then I wonder if the cost is too high."

Paul set the journal down. His mind was filled with pictures of the battle. He could hardly believe his father had been in the middle of it.

His father never talked about the battles he'd fought. Paul had never been curious about them before. The war was always just something that kept his father away from the family. He'd thought his father liked war.

The next day after school while Paul scrubbed old ink from the type at the print shop, he watched his father. Blue-black inky water splashed about the floor as Paul worked the stiff brush across the metal letters.

As usual, men from town stopped to chat while Father worked, wanting to know the latest news. They always had an opinion about it, and so did Father.

Paul tried to imagine him with a musket, aiming at another man's chest. He couldn't picture it. His father, the man throwing the handle of the printing press while he laughed and joked with his friends couldn't have been so fierce.

And yet—Paul's hands stopped scrubbing, and he stared at his father—and yet, when his father came home from war the last time, his uniform sleeve had been almost cut off by a Redcoat's bayonet.

When he was done cleaning the type, Paul walked over to the wall covered with papers telling of the many battles. There wasn't one of Bunker Hill. The British soldiers had still been stationed in Boston then. They only allowed one newspaper to be printed, a newspaper printed by a Loyalist.

When his father's friends left, Paul screwed up his courage. He handed a dampened paper to his father and asked, "What was it like in the war? What is it like to fight?"

His father studied him curiously. Then he shrugged and went back to working the press. "It was war. A man did what he had to do."

"But what was it like in battle? Was it scary?"

"Usually there wasn't time to be scared."

Paul dampened more paper. "What was it like when. . ."

"Father, look at this newspaper!" Joel burst through the door waving a sheet of paper. "Look what they did at the top! Can you teach me how to make a picture like this?"

Father glanced at the picture of ships fighting in the West Indies. "We've printed pictures in the *Boston Observer* before, Joel."

"Not like this one. How do you print pictures?"

Father patiently explained to Joel that the picture had to be made of metal before it could be printed.

Paul's spirits sagged as he listened. His father would rather talk about printing with Joel than about something as important as fighting battles with Paul. Sadness swelled through his chest.

Paul glanced across the press, where James was pulling the wooden handle that brought the screw down on the paper. James smiled at him and winked. Paul smiled a little smile back. It was too much effort to smile a big smile. His father would never like him as much as Joel.

"Would you hang the papers for me?" James asked.

Paul grabbed the paper pole leaning against the wall. The pole was longer than his father was tall. On the end was a short rod that made the pole look like a capital "T." James laid the damp paper that had just been printed over the rod.

Paul held the pole way up, almost to the ceiling, and slipped the paper carefully from the rod onto a round piece of wood that went from one wall to the other. By the time they were done with the paper, the ceiling would be almost covered with papers hanging to dry.

He glanced over at his father, who was still laughing and teasing with Joel. Fear squeezed at his heart. Would his father reenlist? If he did, would he fight in more battles? Maybe this time he wouldn't come home. Maybe his father would die like all those men at Bunker Hill.

Fall passed without Paul's father reenlisting. Instead, good news had been sent in a letter from Ben Franklin to the colonies. The peace talks were going well.

"Why is war so easy to start and hard to stop?" Paul asked his father one evening while he whittled at a new ship in front of the fireplace.

Father grinned. "For the same reason it's easy to start fights with boys at school and hard to become friends again afterward."

Did Father know about Andrew? Paul wondered. But he didn't ask, and his father didn't mention the bully.

Paul snuck away to read the journal whenever he found the chance. It didn't seem like the man who wrote the journal and his father were the same person. Paul felt he knew and liked the man who wrote the journal. He wondered if he'd ever know the man who lived with them.

CHAPTER 8
Victory!

Father seemed to blow into the house on the tail of the March wind. The house shook when he slammed the heavy front door. Out in the kitchen, Paul could hear his steps coming through the house. "Eliza! Eliza, where are you?"

Paul, Joel, and Mother stared at each other in surprise. A moment later, Father burst into the kitchen. He barely glanced at the boys. "The post rider brought a letter from Henry Knox. You won't believe what's up now, Eliza!"

Paul and Joel exchanged excited looks. Henry Knox was called General Knox by most of the world. He used to own a bookstore in Boston and was a good friend of their father's. Now he was one of General Washington's most valuable men. He was in charge of the Continental army's cannons.

Mother stirred the stew simmering in the big black kettle that hung over the fireplace, one hand holding her skirt back so it wouldn't catch on fire. "Calm yourself, William."

"Calm myself? This isn't news to calm a man!"

"What does Henry say?" she asked.

"There's an article passing among Washington's troops. The men who wrote it were too cowardly to sign their names. And no wonder!" He stormed back and forth, waving the paper.

Paul held his breath. He'd never seen his father so angry!

"What does it say, Father?" Joel asked.

"It says since the troops haven't been paid, they should cross the Appalachian Mountains and start their own country!"

"What?" Mother spun about, the dripping wooden spoon in her hand.

"Can they do that?" Paul asked.

"That's not all!" Father continued, his brown eyes flashing. "If they don't start a new country to the west, the article urges them to take the United States by force!"

"They can't be serious!" Mother said.

Paul stared at his father, his thoughts racing. Would there be more war?

"Are the troops truly so angry they would do such things?" Mother lowered herself on the high-backed settle, her hands clasped tightly in her lap.

Paul could see fear tighten her face. Fear began wiggling through him, too.

Father paced back and forth. "They say no one cares that they risked their lives to give the people in America freedom from Britain's slavelike laws. They believe by not paying them, Congress and the states are saying, 'Go starve and be forgotten.' "

"Does Henry say what General Washington plans to do? I can't believe Washington would go along with such plans."

"Washington has already told the men their plans are unthinkable, that no honorable soldier would do such things. Henry believes the trouble has passed, but the troops are still angry."

"How could the soldiers who fought so bravely at Bunker Hill and Trenton think of fighting American citizens?" Paul asked. "They believed in liberty so much that they fought without ammunition and in the snow without shoes."

Father dropped onto the settle beside Mother. "The soldiers think about such things because they are hurting. They've tried to tell Congress and their own state governments that they need the money they were to be paid for fighting. They left jobs to fight. They need money to feed and clothe themselves and their families."

"The soldiers have been angry before this. You're always writing articles about it," Paul said.

Father gave him a strange look. "I didn't think you noticed. The soldiers have been angry a long time, but they kept hoping Congress would somehow find a way to pay them. Now they are afraid that peace will come and that they'll be sent home and never paid."

All Boston was excited that peace was closer than ever. There had been an article in the *Boston Observer* repeating a speech by King George III. He'd finally admitted the thirteen colonies had become thirteen independent countries, and he was going to put that into the peace treaty.

People who had heard his speech in England said that when King George came to the word "independent," he stopped his speech. It was many minutes before he could make himself say the word that meant the colonies were no longer part of his country.

"Aren't the soldiers promised a bonus if they stay to the end of the war?" Mother asked.

"Yes, eighty dollars."

"But that's not even enough for a pair of shoes!" Paul exclaimed. "It takes one hundred Continental dollars to buy shoes."

"That's right." Father leaned the back of his head against the settle. "The states have to learn to work together so they can find ways to meet their responsibilities, like paying the troops. The states have to start acting like brothers," he leaned forward, grinning, and rubbed the boys' heads with his knuckles until they ducked away. "They have to start acting like brothers instead of separate countries."

"What if they don't?" Paul asked.

Father sighed. "If they don't, we'll lose everything we fought for in the Revolution."

That night Paul couldn't sleep. When everyone else was in bed and Joel was breathing deeply beside him, he took the bedside candle and snuck up to the attic.

Ever since his father had told them about the angry soldiers, Paul had been trying to remember a story he'd heard about the troops many years ago, something that happened when he was only four. He paged through his father's journal, looking for it. There it was! Valley Forge!

"January 1, 1778. The past year has been a hard one for General Washington. After our victory in Trenton on Christmas of 1776, when we captured one thousand soldiers and lost only five men, we won only one battle in all of 1777.

"I remember the bloody footprints that marked our path through the snow as we marched to the battle of Trenton. A great many of our men remain without boots or shoes. My own are nearly worn through.

"Peter, who saved my life in a battle last year, has had no soles on his shoes for a month. He has tied the shoe tops onto the bottom of his feet with pieces he's torn from his blanket. The tops are now useless for even that purpose. Today he boiled what is left of them to make a broth and shared the broth with the rest of the men in the tent. It is all we've eaten in four days. I've yet to hear a soldier complain.

"January 21, 1778. We've been in this miserable place for over a month now. In that time, we've built about seven hundred log huts: sixteen feet long, fourteen feet wide, and six feet high. No windows, which makes them easier to heat, but no floors, either. They are dark, smoky places, but they keep out winter's cold. Each cabin sleeps twelve men. We need three hundred more huts.

"At least the exercise of cutting trees and building the huts helped warm us."

Paul remembered that armies didn't fight often in the winter. Spring and summer were the fighting months.

"My respect for General Washington grows," the journal continued. "A local Quaker offered his home for Washington's headquarters. He stays in his leaky tent, like the rest of the army. He says he shall not leave his tent until every one of his men has moved into a log hut.

"I have never seen men in such desperate straits. Even officers often wear blankets instead of cloaks over their uniforms. So many soldiers were cutting up their tents to make clothing that General Washington made it a crime to do so.

"Many nights I haven't worn my coat at all. It's become a common sentry coat. When a man goes on guard duty, where he is without shelter, he wears my coat. When the guard changes, the coat changes with it.

"February 8, 1778. Daily, men die from sickness or the cold. Peter, who shared his shoe-leather broth with us, had a leg amputated yesterday. It had grown black from frostbite."

A lump throbbed in Paul's throat. He ached at the thought of the things his father had seen and hadn't been able to change.

"February 15, 1778. A package arrived from Eliza, with mittens, socks, and a new shirt. My little cousin Maggie knitted some of the mittens and socks. A red-hot Patriot, that girl! I kept one pair of each and gave the rest away. The shirt was like a miracle. I gave my own away only yesterday to a man in the next tent who had neither shirt nor coat left.

"February 16, 1778. I came on an unusual sight today. I was gathering kindling in the woods near Washington's headquarters. He moved into the Quaker's house when the huts were done. I heard Washington's familiar calm voice and followed it. He was alone, kneeling in the snow, praying for his troops and asking God to give him wisdom in leading his men.

"February 20, 1778. A committee from the Congress visited camp. They were shocked at conditions here. Rumor says General Washington has written Congress many times, begging them to send food and clothing. They thought he exaggerated and sent only paper money. There is little food or clothing to buy in the area. The English army is spending the winter only fifteen miles away in Philadelphia. Their gold buys the necessities our worthless paper money cannot."

Paul laid the journal aside. It was growing late, and his eyes were blurring. He started to get up, hesitated, then knelt beside the round-topped trunk.

"Squeak!"

His faithful little mouse friend peeked at him over the top of a broken chair.

"If a brave soldier like General Washington can ask God for help in the war, I can pray, too," Paul whispered to the big-eared mouse.

The wooden floor was hard beneath his knees, but at least it wasn't snow, he thought. "Father God, I don't have anything as big as a war to pray for, and I'm not an important general, but would You help me? Would You make my father love me and help me love him the way I should? If You have the time, that is. In Jesus' name, Amen."

"Hear ye, good men and women of Boston! Hear ye!"

The crowd gathered in King Street quieted at the call from the man on the town house balcony. A ribbon of excitement filled Paul. Why had the people of Boston been called by church bells and town criers to meet here?

On the state house balcony stood John Hancock and the sheriff. Mr. Hancock was the governor of Massachusetts now. The governor wouldn't come out if it weren't important!

"Papa! I can't see!" Davey yanked at Father's breeches, accidentally pulling the tie from the buckle that secured the breeches below the knees.

Paul, Maggie, and Uncle Ethan chuckled. Father pulled up the knee-high sock that had fallen, tucking it beneath the bottom of his breeches leg, and redid the buckle. Then he lifted Davey and settled him on his shoulders. Davey threw his arms around Father's hat, knocking it over his eyes. This time everyone around them chuckled.

It had taken a year and a half, Paul thought, but Davey finally trusted and liked his father. A pain flashed through Paul's chest. He missed having Davey seek him out all the time. Sometimes, he even wished he liked his father as much as Davey did.

April sunshine shone down on the sheriff standing on the balcony. "Good people of Boston, this morning the following very important message from the Congress was delivered to the Honorable Governor John Hancock. The preliminaries to a General Peace were signed in Paris on January 20 between Great Britain, France, Spain, Holland, and the United States of America. Fighting was to cease on this coast on March 20."

Cheers erupted from the crowd. Three-corner and two-corner hats filled the air, Father's and Uncle Ethan's hats among them. Men swung their wives and children around in circles. Maggie grabbed Paul's hands and started jumping up and down. Someone started singing "Yankee Doodle," and the rest of the crowd joined in.

Paul yanked on his father's arm and yelled, "Does that mean the peace treaty has been signed?"

Father shook his head. "It means the people writing the treaty have agreed on what each side will get or give up. Now the Parliament in England and Congress in America will vote whether or not to ratify, or agree to, the treaty."

Davey teetered on Father's shoulders and clutched at his hat. Father put him down. Looking around, Father said, "This is the perfect place to hear there will be no more fighting. It was right here the Boston Massacre took place."

"That was the night I was born!" Maggie grinned. "Thirteen years ago last month."

"Father and our Uncle Stephen saw the Boston Massacre," Paul said.

"And my little brother wouldn't have if it weren't for Maggie," Father recalled.

"Me?" Maggie's eyebrows rose in surprise.

"Yes. He went looking for Uncle Cuyler to help with your birth because he's a doctor."

Maggie's jaw dropped open. "Uncle Cuyler, the Loyalist who lives in New York now?"

Father nodded.

Maggie looked at her father. "Is that true?"

"Yes. You and your mother might have died if it weren't for Uncle Cuyler."

"No one ever told me." Maggie frowned, and Paul wondered what she was thinking.

"I guess the Boston Massacre excitement put other things out of our minds about the night you were born," Uncle Ethan said. "Some people believe the Revolution started that night, not in Lexington five years later."

Paul felt strange inside as he studied his father. Father had been involved in so much of the war. For Paul, the war had been far away most of his life. There hadn't been fighting around Boston since General Washington had chased the British army and fleet out of town in 1776, before Paul was three years old.

Will I ever have to choose whether to fight in a war? Paul wondered. *Would I leave my little boy in order to fight, like Father did?*

When the crowd had finally quieted down enough for the sheriff to be heard again, he read the terms of the General

Peace. People were delighted that the king had agreed to the states' independence. Twice during the early years of the war, Britain had offered peace to the states without independence. The states had said no.

What would have happened if they had said yes? Paul wondered. They might still be part of Britain!

Under the treaty, England was granting a huge amount of land to the new states. From Georgia in the south to the Great Lakes in the north, from the Atlantic Coast to the Mississippi River.

"I declare," called Governor Hancock from the balcony, "that May 15 will be a day of fasting and prayer, a day to thank God for ending the many years of fighting."

"And to ask His guidance in building the new house that is our country," Father added under his breath.

Uncle Ethan smiled at him. "At least the United States of America shall never again have any king but King Jesus."

CHAPTER 9
Charles Returns

"I'm winded!" Paul flopped on the floor in front of the parlor fireplace one spring evening a few weeks later. He and Joel had been playing war with some neighbor boys. They were out of breath and sweaty from the battles they'd fought with the wooden muskets Paul had carved.

Joel flopped down beside him.

Paul rolled over on his back, threw both arms out, and stared at the wall above the fireplace. His ship from Uncle Ethan still sat on the mantle. Above it hung his father's rifle from the war.

Paul got up and hauled his mother's wing chair close to the fireplace.

"What are you doing?" Joel asked.

"I want to see Father's musket."

Joel jumped up. "He'll be mad!"

"I won't hurt it. I want to see what it feels like to hold it. Don't you?"

Joel nodded.

But when Paul lifted it out of the brackets holding it in place, he couldn't hold it. "Help!" He clutched the metal barrel. The stock swung toward the ground.

Joel grabbed it. "Oof!" He dropped to his knees, still holding the wooden end.

Paul climbed down. "Let me try holding it." With a struggle, he lifted it to his shoulder. One hand held it beneath the brass lock and the other reached as far out as he could along the barrel. The musket still swung toward the floor.

"What do you think you're doing!"

Paul almost dropped the musket again at his father's roar. He glanced up. Father's brown eyes were smoldering with anger.

"We. . .that is, I only wanted to look at it, sir," Paul said in a low voice.

Father grabbed the barrel and pulled it away from him. "It's not a toy. Muskets are dangerous. You're never to touch a real gun again unless I give you permission. Do you understand?"

"Yes, sir."

"Joel?"

"Yes, sir."

"It. . .it was my idea," Paul said. *Wouldn't you know I'd find another way to make Father angry?* he thought.

Father surprised him by chuckling. "No wonder you had a

hard time holding it. It's nearly as long as you are tall."

His father held it easily, Paul noticed. Father looked at the rifle almost fondly. "We've been through a lot together."

"How fast can you load and shoot it, Father?" Joel asked, his brown eyes wide with excitement.

"Haven't shot it since Yorktown, a year and a half ago, so I'm rusty. Used to manage it in fifteen seconds."

Paul and Joel exchanged wide-eyed looks. "That's fast!" Paul said.

"We learned at Valley Forge. A Prussian general came from Europe, recommended by Ben Franklin, and volunteered to serve with General Washington. He had us up every morning before dawn, drilling."

Paul remembered reading in his father's journal about what poor shape the army had been in at Valley Forge. "He must have been a mean general, to make sick, starving men with hardly any clothes go out in the snow before the sun was even up to practice."

Father smiled and ran a hand over the rifle barrel. "He could yell something fierce, but he wasn't mean. I believe God sent him to us."

"Why?"

"We needed his training. By the time he got done with us, we were as good as the best European army. We were still cold, tired, and hungry, but we felt good about ourselves because we knew we were good soldiers thanks to him."

"It was awful at Valley Forge, wasn't it?" Paul asked.

"Yes. But it was the hardships that made us work so hard to be good soldiers."

"How good were you?" Joel asked with a teasing smile.

"So good that General Washington chose the Valley Forge

men to fight the hardest battles for the rest of the war."

Paul touched the carving on the maple rifle butt. "Would you show us how to shoot it?"

Father agreed. He slipped his leather cartridge bag over his shoulder, and they went back to Frog Pond, where he could shoot without worrying about hitting anyone.

"I'll give the orders the officers give for each step before I do it," Father explained. He opened the small metal pan above the trigger.

"Handle cartridge!" he called in a bossy voice. He jerked open the leather pouch hanging at his side, pulled out a cartridge bullet and powder wrapped in paper and bit off the end.

"Prime!" Father shook powder from the cartridge into the priming pan.

"Shut pan!" As he shut it he said, "Mustn't get rain, snow, or sweat into the powder, or the musket won't fire."

"Charge with cartridge!" He shook the rest of the powder in the cartridge down the end of the barrel and dropped the cartridge paper with its musket ball in after it.

"Draw rammers!" He pulled off a rod that was attached to the barrel.

"Ram down cartridge!" He shoved the rod down the barrel.

"Return rammers!" Attaching the rod to the barrel again, he said, "If you lose your rammer, you won't be able to fill your musket for another round. Then, too, in the midst of battle it's easy to get in such a hurry that a soldier fires without removing the rammer. The musket will fire a rammer once, but it can't be used again."

"Cock firelock!" There was a "click" as he cocked the musket.

"Make ready!" Father held the maple musket butt against his

shoulder. "Take aim!" He looked down the three-and-a-half-foot barrel.

"Fire!" Paul jumped and Joel clamped his hands over his ears as Father pulled the trigger. Father's shoulder jerked back. Smoke poured out of the musket in a cloud. The air smelled like hot metal.

"That took more than fifteen seconds!" Joel grinned, teasing his father.

Father grinned back. "I'm out of practice. We trained until we could fire fifteen shots in three minutes and forty-five seconds."

"What were you aiming at?" Paul looked around. "I didn't see your shot hit anything."

"Muskets seldom hit what they're aimed at, unless the target is within fifty yards. Speed is more important than aim. The enemy usually comes at you in a line, shoulder to shoulder. If you shoot toward their line, you're apt to hit something."

He means someone, Paul thought, feeling slightly sick to his stomach.

"Want to try it, Paul?" Father loaded the musket, then handed it to Paul.

Paul remembered how heavy it was and was ready for its weight this time. He didn't embarrass himself by dropping the musket, but he couldn't hold it still and straight.

Paul bit his lips and tried harder to hold the barrel steady as he pulled the trigger. The force of the shot knocked him backward, and he landed on his bottom. "Oof!" The musket landed beside him.

His face grew hot from hurt pride when he heard Joel laughing.

Father chuckled. "That happens to a lot of men the first time."

Next Joel tried. He ended up on his bottom, too. Now it was Paul's turn to laugh. Joel laughed just as hard at himself as

Paul and their father did.

Paul and Joel were each allowed to take another shot. "Want to try to load this time, too?" Father asked. Each of them agreed eagerly.

Paul was the first to try. Father gave the officer's commands, and Paul tried to remember what each meant. "Handle cartridge!" Paul pulled a cartridge from the leather bag that bounced against his knee. He bit off the top of the paper the way his father had.

"Aaaugh!" Gunpowder filled his mouth. He spit it out. Then he yanked the back of his hand across his tongue. His mouth still tasted like metal.

His father's brown eyes danced. "Can't help but get the nasty stuff in your mouth."

The musket was too heavy for Paul to hold while he loaded it, so his father held it for him. This time when he pulled the trigger, he knew what to expect. He still stumbled, but he didn't fall or drop the musket.

"Well done, son!"

His father's praise warmed Paul's heart.

Father was hanging the musket back over the fireplace when the front door slammed open and Maggie ran into the parlor. Her cheeks were flushed pink, her eyes sparkling. Her bonnet was barely hanging onto the back of her head.

"Charles is home from New York!"

Maggie's older brother, Charles, had been released in New York along with other prisoners of war who had been held in the prisoner-of-war ships off Long Island.

Now that he was back home, the family met at Uncle Ethan's for dinner. Everyone wanted to know what Charles had seen and heard on his trip.

Charles shook his head. "I think the Loyalists have it worse than the prisoners of war. At least the prisoners have homes to go back to. The Loyalists aren't welcome in the towns they spent their lives in. Their property has been taken away by the Americans."

"Last week at our town meeting, people voted not to let Loyalists move back to Boston," Paul told him.

"Britain has offered them five hundred acres and tools to work the land if they move to Quebec or Nova Scotia. Already thousands have left New York for those northern lands. New York's streets are filled with belongings people are trying to sell that they can't take with them. The wharves are crowded with refugees waiting for passage."

Uncle Ethan set down his crystal goblet. "Some of the refugees are traveling on our ships."

Paul shivered. "I wouldn't want to move to Quebec or Nova Scotia. Winters are cold there!"

Maggie brushed a curl behind her shoulder and lifted her chin. "I think all the Loyalists should be sent to the frozen north. They don't deserve any better!"

"Now, Maggie." Uncle Ethan looked at her beneath shaggy brows. "If all the Loyalists were chased from the thirteen colonies. . ."

"States," she interrupted.

"If they're chased from the states," he continued, "our new country is going to lose a lot of good businesspeople, talented and educated people."

"Your father is right," Paul's father agreed. "If we're going to build a strong new country, we need all the intelligent people we can find to help us."

Maggie set her silver fork on her china plate with a small clatter. "Loyalists can't be very smart. If they were, they would have been Patriots!"

Everyone burst out laughing, even Charles. Paul thought Charles probably hadn't laughed much during his years as a prisoner.

Maggie wasn't trying to be funny, though. Paul knew she meant what she said. She was as opinionated as his father. Father told everyone exactly what he thought, but unlike Maggie, he listened to other people's opinions.

Except mine, Paul thought.

Uncle Ethan laid an arm across the back of Charles's chair. "My son will be joining me in my business." He beamed at the family seated around the table.

A wave of sadness rolled over Paul. His own father didn't want him to spend time at the shipyard, and now Uncle Ethan would have Charles at his side. Maybe Uncle Ethan wouldn't want Paul around much anymore, either.

Family filled the room, but Paul had never felt so lonely.

Trouble with Andrew

Prisoners of war weren't the only ones coming home. In June, Congress told most of the soldiers to go home. They were given only a small amount of the pay owed them. "Get the rest from the states you live in," they were told. Father didn't think the states could afford to pay the men.

The soldiers were allowed to keep their muskets. "A musket won't buy a soldier much food or clothing for himself or his family," Father wrote in the *Boston Observer*.

Soon Boston's streets and wharves and shipyards were filled with former soldiers looking for work. There weren't enough jobs for everyone. Many of the men hadn't much training in any kind of job other than fighting a war.

Every day men stopped by the print shop, asking for work. Father hated to turn them away. He tried to slip a bit of money into the hands he shook as the men left the shop.

One day, as a young man of about eighteen left, his face dejected, James said quietly to Paul, "If it weren't for your father, that could have been me."

"What do you mean?" Paul asked.

"My father and yours fought alongside each other. My father was shot in a battle. Before he died, he asked your father to look after me and my mother."

"I didn't know that!"

"You were pretty young at the time. I was only twelve. I was so mad at the redcoats for killing my father that I wanted to lie about my age and run away to join the army."

"Why didn't you?"

"Your father told me I was the man of the house and that there was no one else to help support my mother and younger sisters. He took me on as an apprentice so I could have a trade."

Paul's mother used to tell him, too, that he was the man of their house. He hadn't felt like the man of the house since his father came home from the war.

"Do you ever wish you'd joined the army, James?"

"Sometimes. But if I had, I'd be out of work now, just like all those men who come by here every day."

"Do you like being a printer?"

"Some days I do and some days I don't. Father wanted me to go to the university. I was in grammar school when the war started."

Paul knew boys in grammar school were usually headed for the university, unlike boys who went to his writing school. "Why did you quit?"

"April 19, 1775, the morning of the battles of Lexington and Concord, the school was closed. Mr. Lovell, the teacher, said, 'War's begun and school's done.' "

Paul's mouth dropped open. "You didn't have to go to school at all?"

"No one did. Schools in town were closed until after the British left Boston in the spring of '76."

"Why didn't you go back to school then?"

"With Father fighting, my parents couldn't afford it. And then Father died, and I came here. I rather like it."

Paul didn't like it. He wanted to be in the shipyard. He was almost ten. There were boys eleven and twelve working in the shipyard. It didn't look like he'd ever be one of them.

As the summer weather of 1783 grew warmer and the days longer, the boys spent more evenings at the pond. After spending the winter pulled up beneath some bushes, Paul's raft needed some repairs, but it still floated.

A year had passed since Paul, Joel, and Maggie had lost the raft race to Andrew. Andrew's raft was no longer usable, so he and his friends built a new one. Paul, Joel, and Maggie enjoyed the pond while Andrew and his friends were kept busy building.

"How about another race?" Andrew asked when the raft was ready.

Paul agreed.

"They're still bigger than we are," Joel reminded him as they pushed their own raft into the pond.

"But we're bigger than we were last year," Paul said. "Besides, you don't want him to think we're afraid to race him, do you?"

When they were ready to start, Paul turned to Davey and Rachel. They'd been playing with their little boats at the water's edge. "Stay away from the water until we're back on shore."

It was Paul, Joel, and Maggie against Andrew and two of his friends. They poled off, the rafts side by side. Excitement raced through Paul. "Come on, Joel! Push harder, Maggie!" They all grunted as they pushed their poles into the bottom of the pond.

Paul could hear Davey and Rachel cheering for them at the top of their lungs. It made him even more excited.

"They're moving ahead!" Paul yelled. "Harder! Push harder!"

In spite of Paul, Joel, and Maggie's best efforts, Andrew's raft reached the other side of the pond and the end of the race four raft lengths ahead of them. Paul was quiet on the way back across the pond, but Andrew and his friends weren't.

"You're slower than turtles!" Andrew called.

His friends laughed heartily.

"I knew we wouldn't beat them." Joel's bottom lip stuck out in a pout.

"One day we will," Paul assured him.

They were almost back to the other side when Paul heard Andrew say, "Let's ram them." A minute later, Andrew's raft smacked against Paul's raft.

"Oooh!" Joel's arms waved as he tried to catch his balance.

100

Paul dropped his pole and grabbed for him. Too late! Splash! Joel landed in the water. Andrew and his friends burst into laughter.

Paul and Maggie stuck their poles into the bottom of the pond, trying to stop their raft. "Are you all right?" Paul asked when Joel sputtered his head above water.

"Yes." He started marching toward shore, his wide-sleeved shirt and breeches clinging to him.

Andrew's raft bumped into a large grey rock beside the shore, where Davey was waiting, holding his little ship. Andrew jumped out onto the rock.

"I'm going to go back across the pond," one of his friends said as Paul and Maggie pulled their raft up on the grass.

"Me, too," said the other.

Andrew waved at them. Turning around, he almost bumped into Davey. Davey stepped back quickly, dropping his little ship.

Andrew looked down at the ship and grinned. Then he stomped on it, breaking the mast and rudder. Davey let out a wail.

"Hey!" Paul jumped onto the large, flat rock. "You didn't have to do that."

"He's just a little kid." From the water, Joel grabbed one of Andrew's legs. Andrew started to lose his balance. Paul gave him a shove. Andrew landed in the water, bottom first.

The brothers and Maggie were still laughing when Andrew climbed out of the pond, his red hair plastered to his face. He shoved it out of his eyes and started toward them. Maggie grabbed Davey and pushed him behind her, out of Andrew's way. Paul and Joel took off running across the empty lot.

"Hurry, Joel!" Paul called.

"I'm running as fast as I can!" Joel's shoes made sloshy sounds as they ran.

Paul looked back over his shoulder. "He's catching up!"

A few steps more and Andrew did catch up. He grabbed Joel's shirt and tossed him backward onto the ground. Paul heard an "oof!" when Joel landed on his back.

A minute later Paul felt himself jerked the same way, and it was him saying "oof!" as he landed on the ground and the air was knocked from his lungs. Then Andrew was on top of him, punching at his face.

Joel tried to drag Andrew off Paul and received a punch in the nose for his trouble. He grabbed his nose with both hands, letting out a screech of pain. Paul swung back at Andrew, but his hands only landed on Andrew's chest and arms. Andrew was a lot bigger than he was, and Paul could tell he was hardly hurting him at all.

Suddenly Davey was beside them, pounding his little fists against Andrew's back and screaming, "Don't hurt my brother! Don't hurt my brother!" Maggie dragged him away before Andrew could hit him.

Finally Andrew stood up, panting. "That will teach you not to pick on me." He marched toward the pond in his wet clothes, calling to his friends.

Paul sat up with a groan. He touched his face and discovered his cheek was bleeding. So was Joel's nose.

Rachel stared at them with huge eyes. "You look awful."

"Do you think your parents are going to be mad at you?" Maggie asked.

Paul and Joel looked at each other and nodded. This day was getting worse and worse, Paul thought. First they lost the race, then Andrew beat them up, and now they had to face their parents.

"I guess we should have known better than to push Andrew," Paul said.

"He deserved it," Maggie said hotly.

That didn't make Paul's face feel any better.

At home, things were as bad as Paul expected. He and Joel sat on the settle beside the fireplace while their mother washed their faces with warm water and their father quizzed them about what happened. Davey hung onto the end of the settle with both hands, listening, his dark eyes wide.

"Well," Paul started, "Andrew stomped on Davey's boat and broke it."

"Yes! He's mean," Davey agreed. "He broke it like this." He stomped his foot against the stone floor.

"Why did he do that?" Father asked.

Paul shrugged. "He likes to do mean things."

Father crossed his arms. "What happened next?"

"Um, Joel and I pushed Andrew into the pond."

"Did you fall into the pond, too, Joel?"

"Yes," Davey answered before Joel had a chance. "Andrew's raft hit Paul and Joel's raft and knocked him into the water."

Paul swallowed a groan.

Their father's eyebrows rose. He looked from Paul to Joel and back again. "Paul and Joel's raft?"

Davey nodded, grinning.

"Tell me about this raft," Father said.

Paul told him. At the end, he said, "We never let Davey or Rachel on it. We thought it would be dangerous for them, since they're so little."

Father nodded. "You're right, it is too dangerous for them. It's also too dangerous for you two without adults around."

Their mother wiped the last of the mud and blood from their

faces. Father leaned forward and looked them over carefully. "I don't think your nose is broken, Joel, but it's going to be sore and swollen for a few days."

He studied Paul's face. "Your face will be so many colors, it will look like a rainbow tomorrow morning." He straightened, shaking his head. "I've seen soldiers after major battles looking better than you two."

"It wasn't our fault," Joel said. "Andrew started it when he stepped on Davey's boat."

"He shouldn't have done that," Father admitted, "but fighting isn't always the answer."

"You fought in the war," Joel said, pouting.

"The Patriots didn't start the war. We tried everything we could to make peace with Britain, except give up our legal rights. When you have trouble with other boys, you should try everything else to work things out, too, before you fight."

"You don't know Andrew," Joel said. "He loves to fight."

"Especially against those of us who are smaller than him," Paul added.

"Some people are like that," Father said, "but you still try." He dipped two cloths into the bucket of cool water beside the door and handed one cloth to each of them. "Hold these on your faces. They'll help keep the swelling down a bit."

Paul winced when he held the cloth to his face.

"You know we're going to have to punish you for this."

Paul nodded glumly, though he thought, *I should think our banged up faces would be punishment enough.*

"To begin with, you'll have to wash your clothes. They're filthy, and your mother has enough work to do. Then you're going to tear apart that raft. I want your promise that you won't build another."

"I promise," Paul muttered.

"Me, too," Joel echoed.

"Finally," Father concluded, "you're not to go near the pond for a month. You and Rachel aren't to go there, either, Davey. It's too dangerous."

"But, Father," Davey wailed, "it's the best place to catch frogs!"

Paul watched his father and mother struggle not to laugh. "The frogs will be a whole month bigger by the time you go back," Father told Davey.

Paul wished he could think of something good about their punishment, but it all sounded bad to him.

CHAPTER 11
Paul Tells the Truth

After school on a sunny, late June afternoon, Paul raced down to the wharf. He clutched his sketchpad with its soft yellow leather cover and charcoal drawing pencil.

He ran down Ship Street, past the buildings lining the harbor and wharves that were filled with barrel shops, taverns, and other businesses that served the sailors and ships. Seagulls hovered above the street or flew down to see if anyone had dropped anything that might taste good.

He hurried past the sailmaker's shop and into Uncle Ethan's

shipyard. He craned his neck to see the top of the almost finished ship in the yard as he walked. Hands grabbed his shoulders from behind. "Whoa, lad! Careful where you're stepping!"

Paul turned around. "Hello, Charles. You've already started working here."

"Yes. Father keeps me pretty busy. Here he comes now."

Paul felt suddenly shy. He'd never been uncomfortable around Uncle Ethan before. Would Uncle Ethan think he was a pest, like his own father always suggested, now that Charles was home? He held his breath, almost afraid to look at Uncle Ethan's face. When he did, Uncle Ethan was smiling like always.

Uncle Ethan clapped his hand on Paul's shoulder a couple times. "Afternoon, Paul. This young man can draw better ships than I can, Charles."

"Is that so?"

Paul flushed in surprise and pleasure at his uncle's compliment.

"Has he shown you his sketchbook?" Uncle Ethan asked Charles. Charles shook his head no. Uncle Ethan raised his shaggy eyebrows. "Will you show him, Paul?"

Hesitantly, Paul handed Charles the book. Charles paged through it. "The first drawings are pretty bad," Paul said.

"But you became better quickly. Each drawing shows progress. Father is right. You're very good."

"Good at what?"

Paul whirled around at his father's voice.

"Drawing," Charles said. "Your son is quite an artist." He handed Father the sketchbook.

Paul wanted to grab it back. His father had seen it before, but he had only glanced quickly at the pictures. Every time he saw Paul sketching, he told him to quit being lazy.

He watched his father page through the book. With every page that turned, Paul felt sicker to his stomach.

Finally his father handed the book back to him. "I've some business to discuss with Ethan and Charles. Why don't you wait for me out on the wharf?"

He didn't say I draw well, Paul thought as he headed down the wide wooden dock. The excitement over coming down to the shipyard had been washed away by his father's arrival. He'd been praying for his father to like him for months now. It didn't seem like God was ever going to answer his prayer. *I can't wait until I grow up and can go away,* he thought.

A merchant ship was being unloaded near the end of the wharf. Sweaty men, some black and some white, unloaded heavy barrels and wooden crates.

Paul found a place out of the way and sat down with his back braced against a barrel. A lone seagull broke away from the many birds circling and calling in the sky above and soared down to land on the barrel. It sat there, cocking its head from side to side, and watched Paul draw. Paul smiled to himself. He'd have to be careful not to set down his charcoal pencil. He'd lost more than one to a curious seagull.

He was lost in his sketching when his father sat down beside him. The seagull flew off, only to return immediately. Father nodded at the bird. "If Davey and Joel were here, they'd try to bring that bird home for a pet."

Paul laughed.

"May I see what you're drawing?"

Paul handed his sketchbook over, the laughter dying inside him.

"You're drawing this ship."

Paul nodded. "It's a new merchant ship from France. I wanted

108

to draw it, so I'll remember how this ship is different from others." He pointed out changes in the lines of the ship.

His father rested his chin on his elbow and listened carefully. When Paul finished his explanation, Father said, "I didn't realize you know so much about ships."

Paul screwed up his courage, took a deep breath, and blurted out, "I want to build ships when I grow up."

"You want to build them, not sail on them?"

Paul nodded.

"I thought you came down to the harbor for the same reasons most boys come, for the same reasons my friends and I came when we were boys. I thought you liked the hurry and excitement. I thought you wondered what it would be like to sail to other parts of the world."

"Well, it would be fun to see other parts of the world," Paul admitted.

"Why do you want to be a shipbuilder?"

Paul looked out at the boats and ships covering the gray water. Little rowboats bobbed in between bright blue and yellow fishing boats. Huge merchant ships with sails so large their masts came from the tallest pine trees in New England's forests brought merchandise from all over the world.

"All those boats and ships started out as pictures in someone's head," Paul said.

His father's eyebrows scrunched together in a frown. "What?"

"When someone tells Uncle Ethan they need a ship, he asks them questions like, 'How will you use the ship? Do you want lots of speed or do you want strength more than speed?' "

His father nodded.

"Then Uncle Ethan makes a sketch of what the ship will look like and how tall and wide each part of the ship will be, how tall the masts will need to be to carry the sails, and how long and large the rudder will need to be to steer the ship. When the sketch is all done, the men in the shipyard put wood together to make his sketch real."

"I never thought of it that way," Father said.

"Then the ship is launched, and it can take people to the other side of the world and back. All because of a picture in somebody's mind." Paul hesitated. "I guess it sounds funny, but I want to see the ships in my mind sailing on the water."

His father shook his head. "It doesn't sound funny."

"Did you have pictures of ships in your head when you were a boy?"

"No. I had different pictures. Pictures of a country where men could choose their leaders and where people had the right to believe what they chose and to say what they believed."

Paul glanced at the black and white men bending beneath their loads as they worked along the dock. "Where people aren't slaves."

"That's part of my picture."

"The new Massachusetts constitution says all men are free," Paul said. "You wrote in the newspaper that some people are mad about that because the people who make laws said that meant black people are free, too."

"That's right. But they aren't free in every state. That's one of the reasons the states can't agree on a way to levy taxes. Now that the states have agreed we need taxes to raise money to pay our debts, they can't agree on how to decide how much each state should pay. Some people want to tax land. Some want to tax the number of people. States with slaves say that's unfair."

"The states are always fighting about something. I'm glad everyone is free in Boston." Paul didn't want to be forced to work in a printing office all his life. He didn't think anyone else should be forced to spend their life in a way they didn't like.

"Father, I'm almost ten. There are boys working in the shipyard who are only eleven and twelve."

"Apprentices, yes."

"Do. . .do you think I could work in a shipyard when I'm done with writing school in a couple years?" His heart thumped so loud in his ears that he wasn't sure he'd hear his father's answer.

Father didn't answer right away. He stared out over the harbor so long that Paul didn't know what to think.

"Are you mad at me, Father, because I don't want to be a printer?"

Father shook his head. "I'm not mad. I spent over six years fighting for people to be free. The Declaration of Independence says God gave all men the right to life, liberty, and the pursuit of happiness. I expect that includes your right to a job that will make you happy."

Paul grinned so hard his face hurt.

"I was thinking," Father said, rubbing his fist beneath his chin, "that we'll have to talk to your uncle Ethan. If you want to build ships, you'll have to do what he thinks is best. To be a shipbuilder, you need to study the science of naval architecture. Ethan can tell us what courses you need."

"Yes, sir." Paul couldn't believe his father was going to let him learn to build ships!

"You'll still be expected to help in the printing office when you're needed. And you may need some more years at writing school."

"Yes, sir." He'd do anything his father asked! "Uh, will you . . .will you talk with Uncle Ethan soon?"

Father grinned and clapped him on the knee. "Within the week, I promise."

A few days later, Paul turned ten. He was surprised when his father said, "I have something for you." He'd never received a birthday present before. It was an expensive carving knife. "For the little ships you like to make," his father said.

Paul thought it was the best thing he'd ever owned. Even better than the ship Uncle Ethan had given him. But better still was the news that Father had talked to Uncle Ethan. Uncle Ethan would arrange for Paul to go to a school where he could learn what he needed to be a shipwright. Later, he could work with Uncle Ethan learning the business.

"Your uncle Ethan said he'd be glad to have such a talented young man working with him."

"Do you think Charles will mind if I work there?" Paul asked.

"It's a big business. I'm sure there will be work enough for both of you."

This is the best week of my entire life, Paul thought.

Another letter arrived from Uncle Cuyler that day. Maggie's green eyes flashed when she told them. "He wrote that he and his family are moving to Nova Scotia, traveling on one of Father's ships. Those awful Loyalists are stopping in Boston on the way and staying at our house!"

CHAPTER 12
A Visit from Uncle Cuyler

All the relatives gathered at Uncle Ethan's the day Uncle Cuyler's family was expected. Charles and Father were meeting them at the wharf.

Everyone else waited impatiently in Uncle Ethan's large, beautiful parlor with its sunny yellow walls and expensive blue drapes and gold-trimmed chairs. Paul was excited to meet the relatives he'd heard so much about, but Maggie was pouting.

"It will be embarrassing to have Loyalist relatives visiting!" She stormed about the room in her best gown, holding the skirt up at the sides so she didn't trip. "What will I tell my friends?"

"Tell them the truth," her father said calmly. "Tell them my brother Cuyler's family is visiting Boston on their way from New York to Nova Scotia."

"If I say they're going to Nova Scotia, my friends will know they're Loyalists. Only Loyalists move there."

"Maggie, I won't have you acting this way in front of Cuyler and Abigail. The war is over."

"Loyalists fought against our army. They fought in the battle where Charles was captured!"

Paul couldn't believe Maggie was talking to her father this way. If he acted like this, his father would take a switch to him.

"The Bible says we're to forgive and love our enemies," Uncle Ethan reminded her sternly, "and that most certainly includes our relatives."

Maggie crossed her arms over her pretty dress, stuck out her bottom lip, and glared, but she didn't apologize.

Paul cleared his throat. "The Declaration of Independence says all people have the right to life, liberty, and the pursuit of happiness. Doesn't that mean Loyalists, too?"

Maggie stamped her foot. "When Loyalists chose to fight for the king instead of the United States, they gave up their right to pursue happiness in America!"

"You shall give up your right to pursue happiness in this house if I hear you say one unkind thing in front of Cuyler's family, young lady."

Paul had never seen Uncle Ethan so mad!

Maggie tossed her curls but didn't say anything.

Just then the sound of the carriage could be heard pulling up outside the front door. Paul, Maggie, Rachel, and Paul's brothers all stood back while the rest of the family greeted Uncle Cuyler, Aunt Abigail, and their twenty-three-year-old daughter Anna.

The younger children had heard a lot about Uncle Cuyler's family, but they didn't know them.

Dr. Cuyler Allerton was long and lanky. Aunt Abigail was short and plump. Anna was short, too, but more slender than her mother. Her blond hair was piled fashionably on top of her head with curls hanging down behind one ear.

"How was your trip?" Uncle Ethan asked.

"Your ship makes for good passage," Uncle Cuyler said with a grin. "And the weather was good, so we made good time from New York. We're glad to be leaving before the winter storms set in."

"They'll have plenty of winter storms in Nova Scotia," Maggie whispered in Paul's ear, "and they'll deserve every one of them."

Paul didn't answer. He wished she wouldn't act this way. She was never mean, except when she talked about Loyalists and redcoats.

Maggie's lip curled. Paul looked around to see what had caused her reaction. His father and Uncle Cuyler were standing with their arms around each other's shoulders. His father waved him and the others over. "Come meet the man who saved me and your grandfather from prison, and possibly worse."

Curious, Paul went forward and bowed the stiff little bow Uncle Ethan had taught him to use when greeting important men. "I'm honored to meet you, Uncle Cuyler."

Uncle Cuyler bowed back, his eyes twinkling. "We've met before, but you're hardly likely to remember, seeing how you weren't even three last time we saw each other."

Joel, Rachel, and Davey shyly said hello to their uncle.

"How did you save Father and Grandfather?" Paul asked.

Uncle Cuyler shrugged. "I think your father overstates the case."

"I do not," Father disagreed. "The Saturday night before the battle of Lexington, Uncle Cuyler told us the British were planning to arrest us."

"Why did they want to arrest you?"

"Because we were telling in our newspaper the things the Patriots were doing and the things the king and Parliament and the redcoats were doing that the Patriots didn't like."

Paul saw Maggie moving closer so that she could hear better.

"Is that why the Bill of Rights says we have the right to freedom of speech?" Joel asked.

"Yes," Father answered. "Since we knew the British troops were planning to arrest us, we left town before they could. We had to sneak out of town, but we made it."

Maggie cleared her throat. "Why did you help them escape, Uncle Cuyler, if you are a Loyalist?"

"We're loyal to God first and to those we love before the king. Still, it was hard to have to choose."

"What would have happened if you'd been arrested?" she asked Paul's father.

"We would have been thrown in prison, tried for treason, perhaps hung."

"Some people let others in their family go to prison," Maggie said, her arms still crossed angrily over her chest. "Charles Franklin's son was in prison because he was a Loyalist."

"Maggie!" Uncle Ethan's stern command made her bite her bottom lip, but she didn't apologize.

"She speaks the truth," Uncle Cuyler said.

Maggie lifted her chin and looked pleased with herself.

"I can understand Maggie's feelings," Paul's father said. "Uncle Cuyler and I used to fight like cats and dogs over politics."

"You seem to like each other now," Maggie said.

Father grinned. "We learned to love each other and respect each other's honesty, even if we never learned to love each other's politics."

The rest of the afternoon, Maggie watched Uncle Cuyler curiously and kept her smart comments to herself. Paul wondered what she was thinking.

After dinner, when everyone was again gathered in front of the fireplace in the parlor, Father said, "Tell us about New York. What was it like living there?"

Uncle Cuyler's smile died. "It's been hard for everyone. In 1776 there was the fire, of course."

Paul had heard about that fire. It was the worst since people from Europe began settling in America. Some people thought Patriots started the fire, but no one knew for sure.

"Once the British troops took New York, Loyalists flocked there from all over the colonies for protection," Uncle Cuyler continued. "There were so many people that huts and tents were all that were available for many of us to live in."

"The rest of the colonies' refusal to send ships to New York with supplies probably made things worse," Father said.

"Yes," Uncle Cuyler admitted. "The cost of the little food that was available sometimes cost eight hundred percent more than usual."

Paul tried to figure that out in his mind. That meant that something that usually cost one dollar cost eight!

Uncle Cuyler sighed. "As bad as things were during the war, I think they are worse now. Thousands are leaving every month for Nova Scotia and Quebec. Uproar and confusion are everywhere. The streets are filled with people's belongings, things they can't take with them on the crowded ships and are trying to sell to raise a bit of money. Not that anyone has money to spend.

117

The wharves are piled high with people and their belongings, too, as they try to get a place on the ships."

Before long, everyone was yawning. While they said their good-byes, Father agreed to take Uncle Cuyler to Cambridge the next day, so he could see Father's younger brother, Stephen. Uncle Cuyler wanted to see the medical school Harvard University was setting up, too. There were only two others in the United States, and both had been closed during the war.

"I'd like to see what's changed in Boston," Anna said. "Maggie, Paul, would you show me about tomorrow?"

They both agreed, but Paul wondered uneasily about how good an idea their planned tour was. Would Maggie be unfriendly to their cousin Anna when she was out of Uncle Ethan's sight?

CHAPTER 13
Sad Good-byes

It was a lovely autumn day for a walk about town. Paul was excited to have a day away from school.

"What do you want to see first?" he asked as the three of them started out.

"Our house and Father's apothecary."

"Patriots live in your house now," Paul said quietly. "And a Patriot shopkeeper uses the apothecary."

"I suspected such would be the case."

Paul thought her stiff little smile looked rather brave.

"Let's just walk. I've missed Boston, though by the time we left, it didn't look anything like the Boston I grew up in."

"Did you leave with the British troops?" Paul asked.

"Yes, in the spring of 1776, after the siege." Anna sighed. "It was harder to leave Boston than to leave New York."

Paul remembered his mother telling him bits and pieces about the siege. After the battles of Lexington and Concord, the redcoats came back to Boston. The American troops, not yet organized into an army, occupied all the land around Boston, so the redcoats couldn't leave the peninsula without fighting. American ships kept many British ships from entering the harbor with supplies for the town.

The British had allowed many Patriots to leave Boston, but Paul's mother had refused. She didn't know where her husband had gone when he left Boston right before the battle of Lexington. She was afraid he wouldn't be able to find her and Paul if they left Boston.

"I remember Old South Church," Anna said, as they passed the building on King Street. "There was a huge meeting here the night of the Boston Tea Party. Thousands were there."

"You were at the Boston Tea Party?" Maggie asked.

"It seemed everyone in Boston was there. During the siege, the church was turned into a riding school for the British troops," Anna told them. "Even though I was a Loyalist, I thought it a shame when the beautiful pews were torn out of the house of worship and horses brought inside to train."

"The streets still seem bare," she said later, as they walked along a street lined with houses. "Almost all the trees were cut down for firewood during the siege. Hundreds of wooden buildings were torn down—first buildings that were falling down anyway, later homes and business places of Patriots who had left Boston. Some of the wharves were torn down and used for firewood."

"People must have been cold," Paul said.

"They always found something to burn. The British soldiers cut down the Liberty Tree. That made a lot of Patriots mad. Many people, even the wealthy, burned horse dung when they couldn't get wood or coal."

"Yuk!"

"Phew!" Maggie held her nose. "That must have smelled!"

Even though Maggie and Paul had lived in Boston all their lives, they hadn't heard everything Anna told them. They were too young at the time of the siege to remember much.

After Maggie and Paul had shown Anna Uncle Ethan's shipyard, the three walked down one of the wharves, sat at the end, and swung their feet over the edge. Water lapped quietly beneath them, seagulls dived and called, boats and ships floated past. The air smelled, as always, of salt, dead fish, and seaweed.

Anna rubbed a hand over the dock's gray, worn planks. "After the battle of Bunker Hill, the British brought back their wounded. There were over eight hundred men. There was no place to take so many men. They were left lying on the wharves all night. I came with Father to help the wounded. So did both of your mothers. The wood on the wharves was covered in blood. It took months for the snow and rain to wash it away.

"I remember thinking the Patriots were terrible people to keep us under siege when there were so many wounded people here."

Maggie shifted uncomfortably. Paul knew it was because she thought Loyalists awful people and Patriots good people.

"Do you remember Dorchester Heights?" Paul asked.

"Oh, yes. That was awful. The Patriots bombed us night and day."

"I remember, too," Maggie said in a low voice. "Not much, but I remember the noise of the cannons rattling the windows, shells bursting in bright lights in the sky, and how frightened I was."

Anna squeezed her hand. "We were all scared."

"How old were you then?" Maggie asked.

"Fifteen," Anna answered. "You were just turning six. Paul was almost three. Joel was only a couple months old. I watched the three of you for your mothers sometimes. It helped me be less scared because I had to be brave for you.

"On your sixth birthday, Maggie," she continued, "we woke up and found the Patriots had built an entrenchment overnight on the hill on Dorchester, across the Neck. The British guards hadn't seen or heard it being built. It frightened the British troops something awful. The British general said, 'The rebels have done more in one night than my whole army would have done in a month.'"

"Father calls Dorchester Heights a miracle," Paul told her.

"Perhaps it was. I don't see how the Patriots could have built the battery so quickly and when both sides kept up a continual firing all night long, and there was bright moonlight.

"British troops couldn't cross the river when they discovered the works, because they'd missed the tide. Later that day they were sent across the river to attack Dorchester Heights, but a sudden, severe storm came up and their boats couldn't land."

"It was Dorchester Heights that made the British leave Boston, wasn't it?" Paul asked.

"Yes. With the battery on Dorchester Heights, the Continentals could hit Boston with their cannons from there on the south and from Charlestown on the north. It was George Washington's first victory in this war, and he hardly lost a man to win it."

"That's why the British called him the cunning fox," Paul told her proudly.

"When the British left, our troops came into Boston," Maggie said. "I remember seeing General Washington." She smiled. "I don't remember him very well. I only remember he was very tall."

"Mother says I saw him, too," Paul said, "and grabbed his coat when he walked by. She says he smiled at me, but I don't remember any of it."

"Did your father and grandfather come back to Boston then?" Anna asked.

"Father couldn't," Paul told her. "There was smallpox in town, and General Washington wouldn't let any of the troops enter Boston if they hadn't had smallpox before."

Anna nodded. "Your mother had the smallpox during the siege but was well by the time Washington came to town."

His mother had scars from the smallpox on her face and hands.

"Boston was a mess during the siege," Anna continued. "It was a severe winter, and we were all cold. There was never enough coal or firewood. Food, either. Meat was very scarce. There were about 6,500 civilians in town and twice that many soldiers. I remember once there were only six steer to supply meat to the entire town. The British troops wouldn't let either of your families buy meat because your parents wouldn't sign statements saying they were loyal to the king."

Maggie looked horrified. "Didn't they have anything to eat?"

"Everyone had some food stored in their cellars, as always, but it mostly ran out before Washington won at Dorchester. Some days we only had a glass of apple cider and a piece of bread. Father could buy meat when it was available and he could get enough money together. When he did, he shared it with your families. He had to be careful not to be caught, or he wouldn't have been able to buy any more."

"Didn't ships bring any food to town?" Maggie asked.

"They tried, but they usually couldn't get through. The Continentals captured the ships or made them turn back before they reached the harbor."

"It sounds like Boston during the siege was a lot like New York when you lived there," Paul said.

"Yes, in many ways it was. Still, it's Boston that's home to me. It will be hard moving to Nova Scotia and knowing I can never come back here to live."

"You could live here if you signed a statement of loyalty to Massachusetts," Maggie reminded her.

"And denied my loyalty to the king of England."

"Wouldn't you be a Patriot instead if you had a chance to go back in time and change your mind?" Maggie persisted. "You're losing everything because you're a Loyalist. You've already lost your house and your father's apothecary shop here in Boston. You've lost friends. Now you have to move to another country."

Anna turned around and looked at the town of Boston behind them, with its tall church spires reaching toward the sky and Beacon Hill on the common rising above all the buildings. "I do love Boston," she said quietly.

"Even thousands of British soldiers are taking a patriotic oath and staying in America. Why won't you?" Maggie urged.

Paul's heart beat a fast rhythm. Would Anna change her mind?

But Anna shook her head. "I believe the same things I did before the war started. The Bible says we're to obey our king and other leaders so we can live in peace. Look what happened when the Patriots didn't obey the king. We all suffered years of war."

"The Patriots won the war. Don't you think God helped them win?" Paul asked.

"Maybe He did," Anna admitted.

"Then why not change your mind and stay?" Maggie asked.

"Because I still believe I'm to obey the king. Besides," Anna smiled, "God must have a purpose for sending so many families to Quebec and Nova Scotia, too, don't you think?"

"I never thought of that," Paul said.

That night when everyone else was asleep, Paul climbed the stairs to the attic again. It was chilly up there in the September evening, but he wanted to know what his father had written about Dorchester Heights in his journal.

Candlelight flickered over the dirt and water-stained pages as he looked for the entry. The journal smelled like old, rotting paper. Paul grinned to himself. His pet mouse would like to feast on this! He'd have to remember to always put it away.

"March 5, 1776," he read. "It is a rainy, windy, cold, and miserable afternoon. The weather has put an end to the constant battery of cannon shells we have heaved upon Boston the last few days and nights. Thanks be to God!

"The flag under which General Washington took command of our army this spring still flies over us. There are thirteen red and white stripes representing the thirteen colonies, but in the corner of our flag is the flag of Great Britain, showing that we are still part of that country. I wonder if Great Britain will want us when the fighting is done.

"Who would have thought when we so eagerly took up arms against the British that we would be firing upon Boston less than a year later! That John Hancock, as president of the Congress, would sign the order for the Continental army to fire on his home, his town, his friends. That Henry Knox, the Boston bookstore owner, would bring the cannons from Ticonderoga that would shell Boston. That he and I and others like us would light the cannons sending shells into the town where my wife and Paul are living."

He didn't mention Joel. Hadn't he known that Joel was born? Joel had been three months old by this time.

"My eyes are gritty from lack of sleep. For days I haven't slept, worrying for my family, wondering whether I've been wrong about God leading our cause. Would God demand this of men as the price of liberty, firing on their own families? Dear God, keep Eliza and Paul and the other townspeople safe from us."

Paul reread the last paragraph, amazed. From the time his father was a boy, he'd been an outspoken Patriot, convincing others with his enthusiasm and words to rebel against the king. Something must have made him decide that he was right to fight. Was it the Continentals' victory over the British at Boston that convinced him? What he called the "miracles of Dorchester Heights?"

Paul's dreams that night were filled with cannon shells bursting in a moonlit night over Boston Harbor.

A few days later, the family gathered on Long Wharf to say goodbye to Uncle Cuyler's family.

"Do you like my hair?" Maggie asked, her green eyes sparkling. "Anna showed me how to do it."

It was styled like Anna's, pulled back from Maggie's forehead and brushed high over a roll. Curls were caught behind one ear and hung down past her shoulders. Paul couldn't figure out why girls were always wanting to change their hair, but if it made them happy. . .

"You look like Anna with your hair that way," he said. It was true. They were both short and had blond hair.

"I'm going to miss Anna. We're going to write to each other."

Paul stared at her in surprise. "But you hate Loyalists!"

Maggie's peaches and cream cheeks turned pink. "I don't hate Anna."

"What about other Loyalists?"

"I still think they should have fought with the Patriots!" she said hotly. "But. . ." She lowered her voice and kicked the toe of her green slipper against a weathered plank. "I guess they had to do what they thought was right."

When they stood waving at the ship carrying Uncle Cuyler, Aunt Abigail, and Anna away, Paul was surprised to see a tear roll down over Uncle Ethan's round cheek.

"We may never see my brother and his family again," he said.

A strange feeling curled through Paul. What would it be like to never see his own brothers and sister again? He didn't know what to say or do to make Uncle Ethan feel better, so he just stood beside him and watched the ship a long, long time, until they couldn't see it anymore.

CHAPTER 14

Caught!

PAUL

Paul liked the church service on Christmas Day. There was the usual Christmas collection for the poor. Then the pastor reminded them that on this day they were celebrating the birthday of the King of Peace, Jesus. They were celebrating peace in the land, also.

But the peace still wasn't final. After dinner, when the family gathered as usual in front of the crackling fire, Paul asked, "The peace treaty signed by England arrived at Congress in November.

Why haven't they ratified it yet? Don't they want peace?"

"Each state is allowed a representative at Congress," Father explained. "All the representatives have to agree before the treaty can be ratified. Some states haven't even sent a representative to Congress this year."

Paul dropped down on the hearth rug. "Why not?"

"We weren't one country when the war started. We were separate colonies, fighting together because we could be stronger together than alone. Some states don't think we need to be one country. Others are afraid if we keep the Congress, it will become more powerful than the state governments."

Paul frowned. "Would that be bad?"

"Not necessarily, but people remember how much power the king wanted, and they want to be sure that no person or group has that much power in our government."

"What if they don't sign it?" Joel asked.

"The treaty could be torn up and a new treaty written, one that's not so favorable to the United States. The signed treaty has to be returned to France by March 3 of next year."

"With winter storms, there's no telling how long it would take for a ship to cross the ocean with the treaty," Paul said. "They'd better sign it soon."

Anger swelled inside Paul's chest. Cornwallis had surrendered over two years ago. His father fought for more than six years to be free from Britain. Now the people of America didn't even bother to sign the peace treaty that gave America the liberty he fought for, the liberty men like James's father had died for!

Mr. Lankford read the Christmas story from the Bible to the family. When he was done, he asked Joel to read a newspaper from New York out loud. "Have to keep practicing your reading."

Joel read an article about the British troops leaving New York.

That was the last place redcoats had been stationed in America. The general had refused to leave until he received a copy of the peace treaty signed by the king of England. He didn't wait for Congress to ratify it.

"As the last redcoats were leaving New York," Joel read, "the American troops hurried to raise the American flag above the fort in New York Harbor. They had quite a time! The redcoats had taken with them the equipment needed to raise the flag. A number of American soldiers tried climbing the pole so they could fly the flag, but alas! The British had taken the precaution of greasing the pole! Before he reached the top, each soldier slid down faster than he climbed up!"

Paul and Joel chuckled at the image of soldiers clinging for dear life to the pole as they slid down.

With the British soldiers gone from America, there was no longer any need for an army. Congress had dismissed the few remaining troops, including General Washington.

The New York paper also had an article giving Washington's speech to the Congress when he resigned. He told them he turned the country over to the protection of Almighty God and the people who would be in charge of the new country.

Paul knew the man who had kneeled in the woods at Valley Forge to pray would continue praying for the new country and its leaders. I will, too, Paul decided.

That evening Paul lay awake a long time. Snow hissed softly as it fell past the window. Finally he stole up the attic stairs one more time. He took a blanket with him for the attic wasn't heated. He'd brought corn kernels with him, as he always did. His little friend's tiny gray head popped up as soon as Paul entered the attic. Paul lay the kernels on the trunk. The mouse squeaked a few times but didn't move to come closer.

Wrapped in the scratchy but warm wool blanket, Paul huddled beside the trunk with the candle burning on top of it and opened the journal. A moment later he heard scratching. Now that Paul was settled, the mouse felt it was safe to eat the corn.

Paul grinned. "You and I have become pretty good friends, haven't we?" The mouse looked at him, but didn't stop eating. He sat on his back legs, a kernel of corn caught between his two front paws, and chewed.

In the past year, Paul had read most of the journal. The entry he read Christmas night was about the battle at Yorktown, his father's last battle.

"In the midst of the fighting, a small British drummer boy in his red coat climbed up on the last remaining parapet and began beating the parley that meant surrender. Soldiers didn't see him, and the fighting went on. The brave boy, alone before two armies, kept drumming. I called for the soldiers about me to cease fighting, pointing out the boy to them.

"But others were still too caught up in the battle to notice. I began to fear for the lad. Then a Redcoat officer climbed up beside him and waved a white handkerchief. The shooting stopped.

"The two walked across the battlefield to the Americans' battle line, the drummer boy drumming all the way. The boy came with a sure step and his head held high, as if he were playing a victory march instead of a surrender.

"There are those who say the war is over this day."

That was the last entry.

Hadn't Lafayette mentioned a drummer boy at Yorktown? Hadn't he said Paul's father had told him there was a drummer boy, a brave lad, who reminded him of Paul?

Prickles ran along Paul's arms. Could this have been the drummer boy Lafayette meant? Did his father think he was as brave as this boy who had stood alone between two fighting armies?

The attic door squeaked open. Footsteps came heavily up the stairs. The mouse darted across the floor and under a pile of old newspapers. Paul caught his breath and stared at the place the stairs entered the attic. Would he be in trouble for being up here?

His father's nightcap appeared first, then his father. "What are you doing up here this time of night?" Father's glance took in the candle, burned low in its holder, sitting atop the chest. "What if you fell asleep up here with the candle burning? Do you want the house to burn down?"

"N. . .no, sir."

Father frowned. "Are you reading another book on ships when you should be sleeping?" He took the book from Paul. "My journal!"

"Y. . .yes, sir." Paul didn't feel like a brave drummer boy now!

"Do you always read other people's journals without asking? Have you no respect for other's privacy?" Father's voice thundered in the low-ceilinged attic, bouncing off the wooden beams.

"I'm sorry, Father. I found it by accident. At first I put it back, but I was curious. I wanted to know what the war was like for you. When I asked you about the war, you didn't want to talk about it. So, I. . ."

"You read my journal without asking." Father sat down on a barrel. He stared at his hands as if considering what to do and then took a deep breath and looked into Paul's eyes.

"I shouldn't have snapped at you. It's only natural you're curious about the war and my part in it. If I were in your shoes, I'd wonder about the same things." He sighed. "It seems I'm always reprimanding you before I give you a chance to explain yourself. That isn't fair to you. Next time I do it, remind me."

"Yes, sir." Paul couldn't imagine reminding his father when he was angry.

"I mean it. I've been away most of your life. Even after being home for two years, I have a lot to learn about being a father." He opened the worn cover of the journal and turned the discolored, torn pages. He took a deep sigh. "I never thought anyone would read this. I put my most private thoughts in it."

"I'm sorry," Paul repeated.

Father shrugged. "Guess a man shouldn't be ashamed of his son knowing what he thought."

"I don't remember reading anything in there to be ashamed of," Paul said slowly.

Father turned more pages, stopping to read a bit here and there. "I wish I had a journal for each of you children. Something to tell me what you did and thought every day for the years I was away. Sometimes I think I don't know any of you at all, and you're the most important people in my life."

Paul swallowed the lump that rose in his throat.

Father pulled an envelope from near the back of the book. It was yellow and torn and folded many times. He opened it and pulled out a paper. A smile trembled on his lips. He handed it to Paul.

Paul looked at it, curious. There was a shaky drawing of a ship on it, with Paul's name in shakier letters.

"I remember when I got this letter," Father said. "You were four. You didn't write anything except your name. Just drew me this picture. I was glad Ethan was looking after you and your mother and Joel, but when I saw that ship, I was mighty jealous of Ethan."

"Jealous of your uncle?"

Father nodded. "I was jealous of the time he spent with you."

Paul didn't know what to say. He remembered when he'd been jealous of his father spending time with Joel. It seemed strange to think of his father feeling that way about him.

"Sometimes," his father continued slowly, softly, "I'm still a bit jealous of him. But I'm glad he's around. Maybe he's one of the reasons you're turning into such a fine young man."

Pride made Paul feel good and embarrassed at the same time. "I like him a lot. But. . ." He took a deep breath. "He's not my father."

Father grinned and winked at him. "You'd rather build ships, though, than put out a newspaper or be a politician."

Paul grinned back. "I sure would."

"Then be the best shipbuilder there is."

"Yes, sir." He glanced at the journal his father still held. "What do you think is going to happen to Massachusetts and the other states? Do you think we'll ever be as big and strong as Britain or France?"

"I don't think God let us win the war so we could fail in building a country. If people keep asking God to guide and bless them and their government, if they quit bickering and work together. . ."

"Like brothers," Paul interrupted.

"Yes, if they work together and support each other, this is going to be a country to be proud of."

"Like a family."

Father nodded. "Like a family. Sometimes it takes a while for everyone to work together, but with God and enough love, people can do anything."

Paul smiled. He couldn't wait to see what the new country would be like.

CHAPTER 15

The Race

In February 1784, a boat finally landed in Boston with the news that Congress had ratified the treaty the fifteenth of that month.

"At last the states worked together!" Paul said to his father.

At the Boston town meeting, people talked about the best way to celebrate. Someone suggested an evening parade with torches in every street and candles in every window. People thought that too much of a fire hazard. They settled for fireworks.

But Paul wondered if the peace was real. The treaty still had to be in France by March 3. Every time there was a storm, he'd stare out to sea. Copies of the signed treaty were being sent on two ships. Would one of the ships make it on time? Would they sink in a storm?

Spring came, and they still hadn't heard whether the treaty reached France on time.

Paul and his brothers were spending time at the pond again. Andrew hadn't outgrown his nasty ways since the year before when he'd beaten up Paul and Joel. He challenged them to another race.

"We can't," Paul said.

"You mean you won't. You're scared you'll lose again," Andrew teased.

"Father won't let us build another raft."

"Aw, poor little babies. Daddy won't let them have a raft."

Andrew's friends laughed.

Paul's ears rang with anger. He knew obeying his father was the right thing to do, but it didn't seem like the right thing when Andrew made fun of him.

He wasn't very hungry at dinner that night.

"Is something wrong?" Father asked.

Paul shook his head and scooped up another forkful of peas.

"I know what's wrong," Davey announced.

Paul groaned. "Mind your own business."

Davey ignored him. "Andrew teased him because you won't let him have a raft."

"Is that true, Paul?"

The whole story tumbled out.

Father rubbed his chin. "You know, parents have been known to change their minds."

Paul stared at his father. "Do you mean we can build another raft?"

"Maybe."

"But it's so dangerous, Will," their mother protested.

"Not if they promise to use it only if one of us is around."

"We'd promise," Paul said eagerly.

"We'd promise," Joel echoed.

"Your mother and I can watch the race," Father said, "and we'll invite Andrew's parents to watch, too. That way, Andrew and his friends won't try any funny tricks like bumping their raft into yours."

"We probably can't win anyway," Joel said. "Andrew and his friends are still bigger than us."

"That might be a good thing. Your raft won't have to carry as much weight as theirs."

Joel sat up straight and grinned. "I never thought of that."

At first Andrew refused to race with their families watching, but when Paul called him a chickenheart, he changed his mind.

"This time we race across the pond and back again," Andrew said.

Paul agreed. "We'll race in two weeks."

Paul sat down with his sketchbook and drew the raft. He tried to think of ways to make a raft that would go faster through the water than their old raft. Then he showed his sketch to Uncle Ethan and told him what he planned to do.

"That's a good plan." Uncle Ethan grinned. "You're turning into a good shipbuilder already. You can build your raft at the shipyard if you'd like and use any tools and materials you need."

Paul chose his wood carefully. He sawed logs in half so that the top of the raft would be flat and easier to stand on. He peeled the bark off the logs so they would move through the water more easily.

Joel helped him hammer the logs together. On the front and back of the raft, they used two small logs to form a "V," like the front of a ship.

"The pointed front will help us move through the water faster than the straight front most rafts have," Paul told Joel.

"Why do you want the back pointed?" Joel asked.

"We have to go across the pond and back. If only one end is pointed, we'll have to take time to turn the raft around before we go back across the pond. With both ends pointed, we can just turn ourselves around, not the raft."

"That's smart! It will save us lots of time."

When the raft was built, they spread brown stuff on the bottom to keep water from soaking into the wood. Davey thought it was great fun helping brush the smelly, sticky brown stuff on the logs. Everyone laughed when he was done.

"You have as much brown stuff on you as on the raft, Davey," Rachel said.

"Next we brush on tallow," Paul told them. "That makes the water flow more evenly over the bottom. The more evenly the water flows, the faster the raft can move through the water."

They put a mast in the middle of the raft for a sail. "We can't use a sail during the race, but it will be fun to have later," Paul said.

Uncle Ethan gave them sailcloth and their mother, Maggie, and Rachel made the sail.

When they were done, their father looked it over. "It looks great! What are you naming it?"

Paul thought a minute. "The Cunning Fox."

They'd learned last year that they couldn't beat Andrew by fighting, Paul thought. He still remembered how long his face had been black and blue from Andrew's beating. He'd learned reading his father's journal how General Washington had been nicknamed the Cunning Fox because he'd won a number of victories and saved his troops by acting smarter than most generals, even when his troops weren't well trained.

If we beat Andrew tomorrow, he thought, it will be because we're using our minds instead of fighting. We'll be making the best raft we can and learning the best ways to sail the raft.

Paul was surprised and pleased when his father painted the name on the side of the raft.

They took the raft in a wooden, hand-pulled cart to a different pond to test. They didn't want Andrew and his friends to see their new craft yet.

Paul poled from one side. Maggie and Joel poled from the other.

Father asked, "Why don't you try it with one of you on each side and one on the back? The person on the back can help the raft steer a straighter course."

Paul took the back. "You're right, Father. This works much better!"

"If you all pole at the same time, you'll go faster still," Father suggested.

The three tried it. When Paul yelled, "Pole!" they all stuck their poles into the bottom of the pond. They kept practicing until they had a rhythm to their poling.

Paul went to the print shop with a smile that day. With everyone working together, they were sure to have their best race ever. Maybe they'd even win!

His smile grew even broader when news reached the shop that the treaty had arrived almost a month late, but Great Britain had accepted it anyway.

Paul handed the broadside to his father. "The war really is over now, and you helped win it." He was so proud of his father that he could burst! Paul could see in his father's eyes the pleasure and pride his words gave him.

"We'd better put the news in the paper and tell the people," his father said.

The war was finally over, Paul thought, carrying in a bucket of water to dampen the papers while his father put together the metal letters. Now if only his war with Andrew could end as well.

Andrew scowled at the raft the next morning, pushing his red hair out of his eyes. "Never saw a raft like that before. Did your father help you make it?"

"No, we kids did," Paul said.

Andrew didn't look like he believed him. Paul was glad Andrew's father and mother were there, so Andrew didn't dare say the mean kind of things he usually said. It was no wonder Andrew was big and strong, Paul thought. His father was one of the biggest men Paul had ever seen and had hair as red as Andrew's.

Uncle Ethan, Aunt Dancy, and Charles arrived with Maggie. Maggie held out a folded piece of cloth to Paul. "Surprise. Rachel and I made this for the raft."

It was a flag, a small copy of the flag that Congress chose for the United States in 1777. It had seven red stripes and six white stripes. In one corner was a large blue square with a circle of thirteen white stars, one star for each state.

Paul grinned. "Thanks, Maggie. Thanks, Rachel." With his father's help, he tied it to the top of the mast.

Paul's heart pounded like a shipbuilder's hammer while he waited, pole in hand, for Uncle Ethan to give the signal to start the race. When the signal was called, Paul pushed his pole against a rock at the edge of the pond as hard as he could.

He could hear the people on shore shouting for his group and for Andrew and his friends. He pushed harder, then glanced over his shoulder at Andrew's raft.

"They're moving ahead! Pole harder, Maggie, Joel!"

"Aren't you going to tell us when to pole?" Maggie called.

Oh, no! He'd been so excited, he'd forgotten. "Pole!" Grunting, he pushed his pole into the bottom of the pond, then yanked it back out. "Pole!"

It took a few calls for them to catch the rhythm and pole at the same time. All the while, Andrew's raft moved ahead. Paul bit back his disappointment. He wanted so much to win this race.

Andrew's raft struck the shore on the far side of the pond. Paul, glancing over his shoulder, saw one of Andrew's crew stumble and almost fall as the raft bounced. Then they were headed back.

"See you on the other side!" Andrew called as the rafts passed each other.

"Watch out!" Paul called as they neared land.

He, Maggie, and Joel each grabbed the mast with one hand to keep from falling as their raft hit shore. Paul leaped to the other end of the raft. "Pole!" They started back across the pond. It took a few hard pushes to get their speed up again.

"We'll never catch them," Joel said, panting.

"Keep pushing," Paul demanded.

A few poles later, Maggie yelled, "We're catching up!" In her excitement, she forgot to pole. They swerved off course.

"Pole, Maggie!" Paul pushed his pole into the water on her side of the raft. After a couple pushes together, they were heading straight again.

Paul took a quick look at Andrew's raft. They were almost even! One of Andrew's friends jabbed his pole at Paul's raft.

"That's cheating!" Joel screamed.

But instead of pushing Paul's raft away, the pole broke.

Joel cheered. "They've only got two poles! We can win easily now."

New energy rushed through Paul's tired arms. He pushed harder, called faster for everyone to pole. In a minute they were a whole raft length ahead.

"My pole!" Joel's voice was high and shrill. "I lost my pole!"

Paul saw the pole sticking out of the water as they sailed past.

"It stuck in the bottom," Joel said, when Paul moved to Joel's side of the raft.

"Move to the back. You're unbalancing the raft."

Andrew's raft was almost even with them again. Paul felt his courage sink beneath the water. He could hear Andrew urging his friend on.

"Pole, Maggie," Paul said, trying to keep their rhythm.

As they neared shore, their families' shouts filled the air, setting his heart racing faster. They swished through the long reeds at the side of the pond. The pointed front of the raft plowed into the muddy ridge of the shore.

"We won!" Joel yelled.

Paul turned to look for Andrew's raft. It took Andrew and his friend two more pushes to reach shore.

Joel pounded Paul on the back. Maggie grabbed his sleeve and shook it. "We won! We won!"

Paul could hardly believe it. After two years, they'd finally beaten Andrew! Their families surrounded them with smiles and congratulations.

Andrew and his father came close. His father's huge hand was on Andrew's shoulder, and Paul suspected that was the only reason Andrew came with him. Andrew's father held out his large hand. "Congratulations."

"Thank you," Paul murmured.

Andrew held out his hand, too, but slowly. "Congratulations," he muttered. His eyes were filled with anger.

"You gave us a good race, Andrew," Paul said.

Andrew's eyes widened in surprise. "Uh, thanks."

"Maybe next time we race, both our crews can keep all their poles."

Andrew actually smiled. Then he laughed. "We'll beat you next time." But his threat didn't sound mean like usual.

When Andrew and his father walked away, Joel asked, "What if we lose next time?"

Paul's shoulders lifted his damp shirt in a shrug. "Then we'll race again." He grinned at Joel. "But I'm sure glad we won this time."

Father rested a hand on Paul's shoulder. "Congratulations, son. You won."

A movement caught Paul's eye. The flag Maggie and Rachel had made waved slightly in the breeze, the states' thirteen stars shining in the sunlight.

"I didn't win by myself. We all won it together."

There's More!

The American Adventure continues with *Adventure in the Wilderness*. Betsy Miller and George Lankford are moving with their families to the river city of Cincinnati, a journey that will take weeks of traveling on ships, wagons, and flatboats. During their trip, they'll explore America's big cities, meet a Native American, foil a thief's plans, and narrowly escape drowning. Through it all, Betsy will continue to wonder if she will ever again see her cousin Richard, who was captured by British sailors and forced to serve on a British sailing vessel.